D0560521

Chasing the Nightbird

Chasing the Nightbird

Krista Russell

PEACHTREE
ATLANTA

Ω

Published by
PEACHTREE PUBLISHERS
1700 Chattahoochee Avenue
Atlanta, Georgia 30318-2112

www.peachtree-online.com

Text © 2011 by Krista Russell

All rights reserved. No part of this publication may be reproduced, stored in a retrieval system, or transmitted in any form or by any means—electronic, mechanical, photocopy, recording, or any other—except for brief quotations in printed reviews, without the prior permission of the publisher.

Cover design by Maureen Withee
Book design by Melanie McMahon Ives

Manufactured in June 2011 in Melrose Park, Illinois, by Lake Book Manufacturing in the United States of America
10 9 8 7 6 5 4 3 2 1

Library of Congress Cataloging-in-Publication Data
Russell, Krista.
 Chasing the Nightbird / by Krista Russell.
   p. cm.
 Summary: In 1851 New Bedford, Massachusetts, fourteen-year-old Cape Verdean sailor Lucky Valera is kidnapped by his estranged half-brother and forced to work in a mill, but while Lucky is plotting his escape he meets a former slave and a young Quaker girl who influence his plans.
 ISBN 978-1-56145-597-3 / 1-56145-597-0
 [1. Sailors--Fiction. 2. Fugitive slaves--Fiction. 3. Abolitionists--Fiction. 4. Conduct of life--Fiction. 5. Cape Verdean Americans--Fiction. 6. Massachusetts--History--1775-1865--Fiction.] I. Title.

PZ7.R915454Ch 2011
[Fic]--dc22

2011002665

To my husband Robby for his unwavering support,
enthusiasm, and editorial advice,
and to my sons Anders and Graham,
who inspire me in more ways than I can list.

Lark's Head

New Bedford, Massachusetts, 1851

If it were true that seagulls possessed the souls of dead
sailors, Lucky Valera wondered which of his former shipmates was diving at him from the June morning sky.

He waved his arms. "Shoo!" His own stomach felt bilgy
for lack of food; he surely hadn't a crumb to offer a hungry
bird. Never mind—by guess and by God he'd be seeing the
last of New Bedford off the starboard stern by noontide. And
with a bellyful of fresh rations in the offing.

He pulled his cap down, hoisted his duffle, and walked
quickly over the dawn-lit cobbles, eager to get to the wharf
where the *Nightbird* waited. Feeling undone as a frayed line,
Lucky yearned to get back to sea. He'd grown up before the
mast and, now that Pa was gone, the ship's hands were his
only friends in this unfamiliar city. And though it was still a
week from his fourteenth birthday, he'd be sailing as full
member of the crew this time, not a lowly cabin boy. He
breathed in the early morning sea air and the smell of whale
oil and tar.

The bird dove at him again. Lucky darted off the street and into the shelter of Spurling's sail loft.

"Is that you, Alcott?" he shouted at the gull. Alcott had made improper advances to the sweetheart of a Nantucket whaleman, and had been ushered to his reward with one quick snap of the whaleman's tattooed forearm.

The gull wheeled, circling. Its wings and body glowed white in the rising sun, but the feathers on its head formed a dark brown hood. Not usual to see a bird like it in these parts, Lucky mused. He wondered if its presence might signify bad luck.

A movement in the shadow of an alleyway caught his eye. A big black cat. Lucky smiled, relieved to see a good omen. The creature padded across the street, staring up at him with unblinking yellow eyes. Between its teeth, still squirming, was a large gray rat.

"Bully for you!" he called after it. "One less vermin on the wharf, one less bunkmate on the *Nightbird*."

He continued down the road, past the mostly dark shop windows and under a succession of wooden signs hanging above the storefronts: a boot, a bottle, an anvil, a candle. Each sign indicated what manner of goods was traded inside. The bakery window cast a lone rectangle of gold onto the street. The smell of fresh bread made his mouth water.

The gull must have smelled it too, for again it appeared, flying low over the shop signs and squawking at Lucky.

He shook a raised fist. "Brownlee, you deck walloper, is that you? You were always the first to show up at ration time." Indeed, it was spoiled stew off the coast of the Aleutians that'd finally done in poor Brownlee.

But the gull didn't answer. It turned and veered off to the northeast.

A woman, broom in hand, stared at him from the doorway of a ship chandlery shop. He doffed his cap.

"Morning, ma'am." She regarded him with suspicion, her glance sweeping the empty street. "Just having a word with a friend," he told her.

The road began to slope more steeply toward the waterfront. Lucky stepped onto one of the iron rails that ran along the side, parallel to the stones. It comforted him to know that just yesterday, barrels of provisions for the *Nightbird* had rolled along these tracks. He wondered what victuals awaited for the first meal aboard. Roast of beef, fried potato, maybe a bit of plum duff? Of course, it would be downhill from there, as far as the quality of the rations. The first meal was always the best.

A shrill screech split the air, loud enough to make his ears ring. Whistles were a bad omen to sailors, and this one bode ill for landlubbers as well, particularly for the poor souls under the employ of the textile mill. The shrill whistle was a muster, tearing the mill workers from their beds and sending them trudging off to the huge buildings that rose from the marshland beside the Acushnet River. They'd labor all day, then lumber home, only to rise again to the same mournful sound, the same dreadful fate.

Lucky shook his head. How could a body tote such a cussed load?

The gull was back. It dove again, this time knocking the cap off Lucky's head.

"Is that you, Caswell, you son of a sea cook? Stealing my gear while you walked in the world of men wasn't enough for you, eh? Back as a feathered fiend to finish your foolery?"

Lucky bent to retrieve his hat. Hell's bells! Could the blasted bird's antics be some kind of a caution? Still crouching, he squinted up at the gull again. "Pa?"

There came a shuffling—the sound of running footsteps on the cobbles. Before Lucky could rise to his feet, a heavy blow struck him square across the back, knocking him to the ground.

"What in the blue—"

His words were muffled by rough canvas as a sack came down over his head. Powerful arms wrapped around his waist, holding him fast.

"Oyyy!" he shouted, thrashing and kicking. "Shove off," he said through the damp material.

It was no use. His captors—he could tell there were two of them—had pulled him to his feet. One held him tight while the other secured the sack around him with a heavy rope.

Awwk, awk, awk. The gull's cry came from close by, sounding like mocking laughter.

"Son of a—" one of the men cursed.

The other guffawed. "Bird sure made a mess of you," he said. "Must have been holding that load for a time! It's all down your back."

"Shut up and move," the other said.

They pushed Lucky between them along the uphill lane away from the harbor.

"What kind of shanghai is this?" Lucky demanded.

In answer came a deep chuckle and a shove to his ribs.

"I'll have you know I'm crew of the *Nightbird*, and no greenhorn!" Lucky said. "Cap'n Butler won't give any quarter when he learns of this gunboat diplomacy."

"That's mighty tough talk for a little nipper," one of the men said. "You can't be more than twelve."

"Sixteen," Lucky managed. The musty smell of the canvas made his gut roil.

"Ha! The lie smells as bad as he does!"

"He's almost fourteen," said the other.

Lucky jerked at the words. How could he know that? Their voices carried the lilt of the islands. Cape Verdeans, he guessed, like his own pa's people. "Lads," Lucky pleaded, "I'm one of your kind, but you've taken hold of the wrong end of the rope. You've got the wrong man!"

"I doubt it. Ain't you that half-pint darkie they call Lucky?" one of them asked.

"Guess this is our *lucky* day." The other chuckled, then coughed and pushed him forward.

"I'm the son of Black Jack Valera, best rigger on the eastern seaboard."

"Heard ole Jack was best at rigging card games. Word is, that's what got him killed."

"Liar!" Lucky couldn't remember when he'd been delivered such a broadside. He sprung toward the hateful voice, his head making contact with what must have been a fleshy belly. He

5

felt the air go out of the man and heard a groan, but he had no chance to revel in satisfaction before doubling over in pain from a blow to the head. A fog descended, muddling his thoughts and finally enveloping him completely.

When he came to, Lucky found himself flung over a shoulder and being carried like a sack of herring, away from the wharves, the harbor, and the *Nightbird*.

He could smell only sour cloth but knew the air had changed. The sounds were not those of the wharves, but the click-clack of hooves and the clanging of steel milk jugs as a dairyman's wagon made its way, with many stops, down a thoroughfare. He must be in a neighborhood.

"Runaway," he heard one of the men say.

"Shanghaied!" Lucky yelled but heard only laughter in response.

Finally, the man who carried him stopped. "Thanks, Antone," he said.

"You owe me," Antone replied from a distance.

Lucky's breath caught. One of them had departed; there might be hope. Despite Lucky's weight, his captor ascended a stairway without effort. He heard a door open as he was lowered to the floor.

"Stand still or I'll box your ears."

Lucky stood motionless while the line was untied and the canvas removed from his head. He blinked and rubbed at his eyes. The air was suddenly filled with a wonderful, spicy smell. An aroma that brought with it the tug of a memory. Island food.

Then Lucky saw him. A large man of about thirty years,

with skin a shade or two lighter than his own, wearing land-lubber's gear with shirtsleeves rolled up to expose muscular forearms. The man glanced down at his biceps, following Lucky's eyes. A self-satisfied smile passed over his face—a visage fierce, terrifying, and yet strangely familiar.

He directed his attention back to Lucky, a sneer lifting one side of his mouth. Finally, his lips parted to reveal a row of small brownish teeth. "I'd know you anywhere. Especially with that ratty old scarf around your neck."

Lucky's nails bit into his palm. He swallowed and the tendons in his neck went rigid, closing the space between his skin and the kerchief, making it feel too tight. He reached up and tugged at it, straightening the knot at the front. It was Pa's spare. Lucky'd worn it every waking moment since Pa's death. Its presence comforted him in a tangible way, as though by wearing it tied securely around his neck, he could somehow gather and hold the memories of his father.

What would Pa do now?

The man gave a disgusted snort, seemingly disappointed that Lucky had failed to rise to his insult.

Lucky was done sizing up the kidnapper; the *Nightbird* would soon sail and he intended to be aboard. His mind had already leapt ahead from whaleman's commandment #3 (fight anytime you think you can win) to whaleman's commandment #4 (run when you know you can't win). This was a case of fish or cut bait, and Lucky would be cutting. Right out the open window to his left, he decided. Probably a ways up from the ground, but it couldn't be helped.

"And you are?" he said, turning his gaze back to the

man's face and its wide, ugly smile. Three strides, he figured, then a leap of faith and—if he survived that—freedom.

"You don't recognize me?" the man asked.

Lucky edged toward the opening. "Why would I? You're obviously no sailor."

"No," he replied, and Lucky caught a glimpse of something dark behind his eyes. "I'm your brother."

Ordinary Knot (seized)

I got no brother," Lucky said. But even as he spoke, he noticed how the dark, almond-shaped eyes glaring back at him resembled Pa's.

"Fernando Fortuna," the man said. He started to extend a hand. Then, as though thinking the better of it, withdrew.

"I got no brother," Lucky said again.

"You do now. I'm Jack Valera's son, same as you."

"Then how come I never heard of you?"

"Guess ole Jack chose to forget." Fortuna shrugged. "Maybe it was easier for him that way."

"How come you don't have his name?"

"Let's just say *I* didn't forget." The sneer on Fortuna's face made him look so unlike Pa that Lucky thought he might be wrong about the resemblance after all.

"Clobbering and kidnapping are mighty peculiar ways to show brotherly regard." Lucky moved several inches closer to the window. "Maybe you're what you say, maybe you're not." He shook his head, wishing he could shake off the confusion that had settled on him like a numbing polar cold. Once he escaped, he'd try to sort out what this all meant. He tried to keep his voice from squeaking. "We ain't got no way of knowing, seeing as Pa's gone."

"So I heard. And what of his pay from that last journey?" Fortuna eyed him suspiciously.

"Spent." Lucky glanced up at the smoke-stained ceiling, trying to keep his temper in check so as not to blow his chance of escaping.

"Too bad I didn't find you sooner."

"What would you have done? Cancelled the marker I ordered and stolen the money?"

"Ah, we come to the point of this sentimental family reunion." The malice in Fortuna's eyes made Lucky step back. "You, little brother, are now in my tender care. Consider yourself under my wing."

"Thanks, but no thanks." Somewhere in the distance, a gull cried. This time, instead of laughter, the calls sounded like mournful sobs. Lucky bristled. "I got by fine before I had any brother, and I expect I'll be fine still. No need to worry any about me. I'll be off now," he said, turning toward the door. "Fare thee well…"

Fortuna leaped at Lucky and grabbed his arm, yanking it behind his back.

"You misunderstand," Fortuna said. "Our dog of a father owes me. Since he's gone, you'll have to pay instead."

"Listen," Lucky said, squirming under Fortuna's grip, "I've no quarrel with you. But I got nothing to do with any wrong done before I was born. Why waylay me when my ship's ready to set sail?"

"Because I can."

"I'll share my take with you, just as soon as I get back to port," Lucky said.

Fortuna's laugh was bitter. "I cut my teeth on a sailor's lies. You'd be long gone before I saw a dime of what you made on that voyage. You whalemen are all alike." He shook his head, a mocking look of regret on his hard, chiseled features. "Slippery and shiftless."

Lucky felt the breath pass hot through his nostrils. "And broadsiding a fella on the street? Is that what you landlubbers call 'above board'?"

Fortuna laughed again. "I'll allow my methods may have been a bit extreme. But I didn't know how you'd react to the news."

Lucky seethed. "You had no right! You can't just pluck a body off the cobbles!"

"Ah, but I can." Fortuna smiled, which made him look like Pa again. "You've not reached the age of majority, and as your guardian—"

"My what?"

"Your guardian. Until you turn seventeen, you cannot work on a whaling ship without a writ that gives my express permission."

Lucky could only stare.

"So you see, little brother, it's true what they say: Blood *is* thicker than water."

"I don't know, Fortuna," Lucky said. "That bilge you're spouting is mighty thick—"

The blow was delivered so swiftly, he didn't even see it coming. It lifted Lucky off his feet and sent him sprawling backward. The thunk of his head hitting the floor was the last thing he heard.

"Lord love us, Beulah, I think the boy may be coming around."

Lucky opened his eyes. At first, he believed himself aboard the *Nightbird*, for the deck seemed to sway beneath him. But the place lacked the comforting smell of sea air. The light was dim, and he couldn't see who'd spoken. His head hurt so much he had to close his eyes again.

A cool, wet cloth came down across his face and the memory of the sailcloth and kidnapping came back in a rush.

"Shush now," a woman's voice soothed. "You're all right. Me and Beulah'll take good care of you."

He tried to rise but the pain behind his eyes had him betwixt wind and water.

"Don't move just yet. Give it a minute." The woman's voice had the same soft lilt of the islands. What was the name of the largest island? *Brava*, Lucky thought, *or Fogo, maybe*. He fought sleep. There was something he had to do.

The ship! He'd miss the ship if he didn't get to the wharf. He struggled to sit. This time, when he opened his eyes, the room appeared in threes around him. Chairs, deacon's benches, and a long table crowded around him. On one side, a fireplace with a large stone hearth took up most of the wall.

A woman leaned toward him, a worried expression on her lined face. Fleshy and dark, she wore a tight red turban on her head and a full homespun skirt with an immaculate white apron.

"Who are you?" he asked.

"I'm Mrs. Cabral," she said. "This is my boardinghouse and your new home."

Lucky shook his throbbing head. "My home is the ocean, ma'am, and I need no other. I best be heading to the wharf directly or I'll miss my ship." He attempted to stand but the floor moved under him again.

"You hear that, Beulah? Boy just got here and he's already set on taking his leave." She tutted and bent over him again.

Lucky peered behind Mrs. Cabral looking for the silent Beulah, who might offer him some help. But aside from the furniture and hearth, the room was empty.

"Can't you see I could use a hand?" Mrs. Cabral turned to face him, arms raised as if to emphasize her point.

Lucky drew back. Yes, the woman could clearly use a hand. A right hand to be precise. For just a slipknot-length below the elbow, her arm tapered off and ended abruptly. She waved the stump in his face.

"Gotcha!" she cried and her face creased. "Look at the boy, Beulah," she said, smiling at her stump. "Don't it look like he's seen a ghost?"

Only a truly demented person, Lucky decided, would carry on conversations with a missing limb, much less give that stump its own name.

A bell tolled in the distance. Two...three...then more.

With each resounding peal Lucky's spirits sank along with his body onto the smooth floorboards. Noon. It was already too late. The *Nightbird* had sailed without him!

"Boy's taken a turn." Mrs. Cabral stooped to put her hand on his forehead.

Lucky brushed it away. "He shanghaied me! How'd you feel if someone you didn't even know kept you from making your living?"

"Fernando's your brother and your only living blood relative. You should be glad he wants to take care of you."

"I don't believe he's my brother. If this knot on the back of my head is what you'd call care, I'll give him a wide berth in future."

Mrs. Cabral chuckled. "He's your brother all right. You two's just alike. He's a little rough around the edges, I'll grant you that. But he hasn't had an easy time of it, coming up on his own."

Lucky was done hearing about that dirty dog. He'd need to get to the waterfront and find another ship. "Thanks for your concern, ma'am. I'll not suffer you any longer." He rose unsteadily.

"Well, I'm sure you will, but that's my cross to bear. You can start with pumping some water so I can wash these floors. Then I'll need some firewood."

"I can't stay here all day and do landlubber's chores!"

"No, that's true. You'll need to go over to the mill to learn the ropes there."

"The mill?"

"Oh, Beulah." Mrs. Cabral sighed. "He hasn't told the boy."

14

"Hasn't told me what?" Lucky asked.

"You may have lost one job, but Fortuna's signed you up for another. You're going to work with him at the mill."

If there had been anything in his stomach, Lucky would have lost it. He tried to swallow the bitter taste in his mouth. So this was why Fortuna had snatched him off the street—he wanted Lucky to be some sort of mill slave. Well, there was as much chance of that as blindly tossing a harpoon into the Atlantic and striking blubber. "I am a sailor," he said. "I can box a compass, tie twenty-three kinds of rigger's knots, climb a mainsail, and put a harpoon into the side of a whale in ten-foot seas. Soon, I'll be the best ship's rigger on the eastern seaboard. I don't do piecework."

"Ha!" Mrs. Cabral smiled at him with a good-humored nod. "That's a nice speech, boy, but your riggin' and whale huntin' days are over. You're a mulespinner's assistant now!"

"We'll see about that," Lucky said. "Where's my duffle?"

"Your brother has it."

The duffle held all of his worldly possessions, including the rigger's knife and tools he'd inherited from Pa. That knife was the only thing of value Lucky'd ever owned. A double constrictor hitch knot formed in his throat. He swallowed hard. "That lowdown, barnacle-scrapin' scalawag..."

Mrs. Cabral cut him short. "In the meantime, I need that water. Bucket's at the back door, down the stairs, to the left through the kitchen." When Lucky didn't move, she prodded his arm with her stump. "Come on, lend us a hand."

Midshipman's Hitch

Lucky rose and made his way past the row of closed doors lining the narrow, whitewashed hallway. He descended the steep staircase, noticing again the smell of Island food. It was chachupa, a Cape Verdean dish of corn, beans, chorizo, and sweet potato. Pa had introduced him to the delicacy last spring when the *Nightbird* had stopped to provision and recruit crew on the tiny rock island of Fogo.

Maybe if he fetched water for the crazy woman, she'd give him a ration. Or should he even be thinking about staying there long enough to eat? He reached into his pockets and pulled them inside out. Tiny bits of lint drifted to the floor, and that was all that remained. His coins were gone. "Hell's bells!"

"Missing something?" He hadn't noticed that Mrs. Cabral had come down the stairs behind him.

Lucky eyed her suspiciously. There wasn't a single member of the *Nightbird*'s crew who hadn't had his pockets lightened in his sleep by a land shark, the name sailors used for an unscrupulous landlord. One thing was for sure, either the one-handed woman or that cutthroat Fortuna had his bag, his gear, and everything he owned in the world but the clothes on his back. *Not for long,* he thought.

"Where's Fortuna?" he asked.

"Said he'd be back in three shakes. Why?" She regarded him with narrowed eyes. "If you're thinking you can light on out of here, you can forget it."

"I'm a fish flapping on the deck. With my duffel and money both gone, I've no choice but to stay on a bit and try to get 'em back."

She nodded. "Them's wise words, boy. No use wasting time fighting the current. Sometimes you have to sail north to get south."

"My husband was a boat steerer," she added, as if reading his thoughts. "Get me that water and I'll serve up some stew."

He picked up the tin bucket and passed through a heavy planked door into the yard.

Divided into quadrants, with the water pump occupying a prominent spot in the middle, the back garden of Mrs. Cabral's boardinghouse would make even the most particular of shipmasters proud. Neat rows of cassava and squash vines, just starting to bloom, snaked out from the dark earth to Lucky's left. To the right, cabbage and turnips grew with young corn plants that came to his knee. At the back of the property, where a decrepit wooden fence separated the yard from the one beyond, beanpoles had been artfully arranged in a crisscross pattern. Overhead, an arbor made of driftwood and barrel stays held an enormous grapevine with new light-green tendrils reaching up to the sun.

The smell of soil, which usually made him feel claustrophobic and uneasy, was instead comforting in its heady richness. Lucky knew more than he cared to know about vegetables. As the cabin boy, he'd loaded bushels of them onto the *Nightbird* whenever they stopped in port—and then spent countless hours peeling and chopping them in the galley.

With a jarring shriek, a gull lighted on the back fence.

"Oh, it's you…" He recognized the brown head against the white body immediately. He owed this bird for trying to belay Fortuna with a heavy load of dung. "You're smart as a Philadelphia lawyer." Lucky doffed his cap. "I think I'll call you Delph." The gull cocked its head and called in a way that seemed to indicate agreement.

"What's keeping you?" Mrs. Cabral called.

"Coming." He hurried along the smooth path toward the house. "Adios," he said to Delph over his shoulder.

Within minutes, Mrs. Cabral had served up the promised afternoon meal and disappeared with the bucket of water. Though he felt a bit disloyal to old Enoch, the galley cook on the *Nightbird*, Lucky savored each mouthful.

"Where's Mrs. Cabral?" Fortuna asked, entering the kitchen and taking a plate from the sideboard. He filled it using a ladle from the pot and took a seat next to Lucky at the table.

Lucky drew his arms in closer to his body. The mouthful he chewed suddenly lost all its taste. When he swallowed, a piece of potato stuck in his throat. "Washing the floor," he managed to say after finally getting it down.

Fortuna took a bite of stew and then another. Soon his

plate was empty. He stood and pushed back from the table, wiping his mouth with his sleeve. "Let's go," he said.

Lucky eyed him over his second plate of chachupa. It had been a wise decision to carry water for Mrs. Cabral. The meal was the best he could remember. Though the food had improved his mood considerably, he wasn't ready to give quarter to Fortuna.

"Where's my things?" he said.

"I'm keeping them for you. Not that they're worth saving. A moth-eaten wool cap and jacket—"

"Those've seen me around the Horn in some dirty weather!" Lucky protested.

"Don't worry, I haven't tossed them on the rubbish pile."

"What about my rigging tools and money? You have no right to keep me from my ship and trade!"

"I have every right. Everything you own is mine. For the next four years, *you* are mine. That's what the law says."

"If it's what the law says, why'd you have to grab me on the street?" Lucky asked.

Fortuna laughed. "Didn't want to take the chance of you slipping away. If you're anything like our father, you're an expert at that."

"Why'd you wait 'til now to make yourself known?"

"Before our father died, I had no claim on you."

Lucky stared at the plate in front of him, his appetite gone.

"So you see, you have no need for rigging tools." Fortuna nodded toward the door. "Dinnertime's over. We're due at the mill."

Lucky turned the words over in his head. He needed fresh air and a chance to think.

"Know this," Fortuna said. "I'll send you to blazes if you don't do as I say. I've already started to sour on your talk of the sea."

Lucky rose and followed him down the hallway that led to the front of the house. A tall hall tree guarded the door, its long arms reaching toward the ceiling. An assortment of hats and caps dangled from hooks like apples. On the lower branches hung a multitude of dark-colored coats and capes. The bottom held a stand containing several walking canes and parasols.

"Whose are these?" Lucky asked. It appeared that at least thirteen souls must have come for tea.

"Boarders," Fortuna said.

"Where are they?"

"Gone whaling." He took Lucky's sleeve and pulled him through the door onto the outside landing. "Or dead."

Lucky wanted to know more, but his half brother was down the stairs and on the street before he could ask. He followed, but turned to take a look at the outside of Mrs. Cabral's house. Its clapboards had once been whitewashed, but time and the elements had left the building looking as if it had been dipped in the ocean and only white salt residue remained in the crevasses.

The yard in front was neatly swept, though, and as he turned to catch up with Fortuna, Lucky thought he saw a movement in one of the front windows.

"Is this the place they call Little Fayal?" he asked.

"You've never been here?" Fortuna said. "I guess I shouldn't be surprised that ole Jack didn't keep with his own."

"Sailors *do* keep with their own," Lucky said. "We bunked at the Mariner's House."

They passed three dark-skinned children, one leading a bedraggled-looking dog by a rope. They stopped talking as Fortuna and Lucky moved closer, and kept the dog out of Fortuna's path.

"Among our people, children are respectful to their elders. You would do well to learn this quickly."

"I'm respectful," Lucky said. He could feel his color rising. "Whaleman's commandment #6 is 'swear, but never in front of a good woman.'"

Fortuna let out an exasperated sigh. "When we get to the mill, just keep your mouth shut." He glared at Lucky. "And tuck in that silly scarf! That gets caught in the machine and it'll wring your fool neck."

Lucky bristled at the insult to the only thing he still had left that was Pa's. He tucked it into his shirt. No use arguing with Fortuna. Instead, he'd try to get on the man's good side. Maybe that way Lucky could find out where the cussed swindler had stashed his goods.

"Look here," Fortuna said, pointing down the street they had just crossed onto. "This is Water Street. You stay on it 'til you reach the train tracks, then go north two blocks to Third Street. Turn right on Third, and you'll be at the mill."

"I know my way around this part of the city. You don't have to tell me how to get there."

"You know your way around the waterfront, you little

wharf rat. I'm telling you that these are the only thorough-fares you are permitted to travel. If I find you've been else-where, I'll row you up the salt river. Understand?"

"Jeesh," Lucky said.

Fortuna grabbed his ear. "And listen good. I've put the word out on you among the merchants and ships' agents. It's on the dossier that you're underage and lack my permis-sion to ship." He twisted Lucky's earlobe viciously. "Hear?"

"Oyyy. Yes." Hell's bells! He'd been counting on Fortuna being unwise to the ways of maritime trade. How'd he found out about the dossier? This would make his lot much harder.

As they neared the corner of Union and Water streets, the sidewalks became more crowded. Here beat the heart of the shoreside district, where Lucky had passed earlier this morn-ing, full of anticipation and blissfully unaware of Fortuna.

Could it have been just a few hours ago? He scanned the faces in the crowd for someone he knew. But they'd all gone. Away on the ship, full up with supplies and hope, into the wide Atlantic. It could be three years or more before the *Night-bird* returned. Never mind, Lucky told himself, he'd just have to find a way to catch up with her.

"Read and ponder, my good people," a man called from a street corner in front of them, "The Fugitive Slave Act of 1850." He held a stack of handbills, which he pressed on passersby. "A law that disregards personal liberty, tramples on the Constitution, and makes criminals of good Christians!"

Fortuna quickened his steps to get past.

"You sir," the man said, reaching for Fortuna's elbow. "Are you already a member of the Abolitionist Society?"

"Why would I be?" Fortuna glared at him.

"As a colored man, I'd think this would interest you."

"I'm Cape Verdean," Fortuna said, his voice low and menacing. "What use would I have for your fool society? Besides, I think personal liberty is overrated." He grabbed Lucky by the ear. "Isn't that true, brother?"

Lucky shook off Fortuna's grasp.

The man's face turned red. "The slave catchers don't care who you are or where you came from, my good man." His voice rose to include the gathering crowd. "You're colored, and as such could be kidnapped and forced into a life of slavery."

Fortuna grabbed the abolitionist by the collar.

Like me! Lucky wanted to shout.

"You can shout from street corners if you've got nothing better to do," Fortuna growled in his ear. "But some of us work for a living." The man's eyes widened. "Do not bother me or my *brother* again." Fortuna gave the abolitionist a shove and the stack of handbills fell from his hand and scattered. Fortuna stepped on several of them as he charged down the street.

The hope Lucky'd felt evaporated like a raindrop on tar. What had he been thinking? Laws made by a bunch of fancy landlubber politicians in Washington didn't have anything to do with him. Bunch of hot air in slack sails.

"Someday," Fortuna said, his mood seemingly improved by his dispatch of the abolitionist, "my name will be known on these streets."

"These streets aren't so fine," Lucky said. "And Pa's name

was spoken in ports far off as Valparaiso, the jewel of the Pacific."

Fortuna glared down at him. "And everywhere else he owed money."

"No! Pa was known as far abroad as the Galapagos Islands, where they have birds with feet bluer than a May sky."

"Probably talked a blue streak of lies."

Lucky bit back the urge to defend his father. He gritted his teeth and kept walking. One way or another, he'd get Pa's knife back.

The waterfront was so close he could smell the whale oil.

Fortuna pointed at a plaque outside one of the bank buildings. "*Lucem Diffundo,*" he read out loud. "Do you know what that means?"

Lucky shook his head.

"I pour forth light."

Fortuna poured forth something, but it surely wasn't light, Lucky wanted to reply. Best keep it to himself.

"Someday, I'll have my share in all this."

This was too much. Lucky couldn't hold back the wave of fury. "Any share you're able to wrangle was born on the backs of men like Pa," he said. "*They* made this port rich on whale oil. What've *you* ever done?"

"Don't forget your own scrawny back," Fortuna said. "You'll have a part in the getting of my fortune."

Weaver's Knot (complete)

"One, two, three, push away, lads!" the foreman called. Down at Merchant's Wharf, a bark was being hove on beam-ends to have her seams recaulked. Lucky stood on tiptoes to see the vessel's green-barnacled underbelly exposed to the midday sun. She wasn't near as fine a ship as the *Nightbird*. He spat on the ground, nearly hitting a lady with a wide satin hoopskirt and parasol.

"Excuse me, ma'am," he said.

She hurried on without looking in his direction.

Fortuna pushed ahead. The crowd thinned when they turned onto Hillman Street, but on North Third, they joined scores of mill workers returning to work from their dinners. Many poured out of modest two-story buildings that stood in rows along the street close to the mill.

Lucky half-considered losing Fortuna in the crowd and running back to the wharves. He could try to find a departing ship and stow away. But he wasn't ready to give up the tools of his trade, Pa's tools, without a fight.

A large group gathered in the vestibule of the enormous

building. The mill was even more imposing up close. The brick façade rose three stories high and blocked even the bright noon sun. Tall windows were menacing mouths with rows and rows of teeth.

To the right, the river stretched and opened to the harbor. A fishing dory, nets hanging at her sides, slid past toward open water. Lucky thought he could hear the tap, tap of hammers as coopers on a distant wharf formed the giant casks that would go off to sea empty and come back brimming with whale oil.

A cold wind blew off the river, making him shiver and wish for his jacket, which was now in Fortuna's possession.

The line moved toward the mill door.

He followed, staring hard at Fortuna, who was in front of him, turned to the side. *Probably watching to make sure I don't run,* he thought. Fortuna's profile did look like Pa's. In fact, if Lucky squinted, he could be Pa.

Lucky turned away, his gaze scanning the harbor. Somewhere out there was a ship aboard which he would escape. He might have to be cabin boy again, but it would only be for a while, until he could find the *Nightbird.*

Fortuna stepped forward and spoke with a woman, and her bonnet bobbed as she laughed at something he said. Lucky moved closer to hear.

"In fact, I was just the other day speaking with my friend, Antone, about the opportunities in this fine city. That is, for a man who's not afraid of hard work." Fortuna caught Lucky's eye over the girl's bonnet and gave him a warning look.

"You've never been one to shy away from hard work and steady habits, Fernando," the girl said. "I just know you'll be successful."

"Fernando," Lucky said, smirking at her use of Fortuna's first name. "Why don't you introduce me to yer sweetheart?"

He was gratified to see Fortuna's eyes narrow menacingly back at him, though he knew he'd likely pay a stiff price later. Never mind. Hopefully, he'd be gone before the scoundrel had a chance to mete out retribution.

The girl giggled and turned. "You must be Fernando's brother," she said.

Lucky stared into eyes that put him in mind of the Sargasso Sea, where green and brown swirled together in a mix of vine and kelp that could stop a ship. Legend had it that if you were entangled, there was no escape.

"You're prettier than all the ladies of Buenos Aires, both fine and fancy," he heard himself say. Horrified, he felt the color rise to his own face and wished he could disappear.

Several people around them snickered. There was a shocked gasp from an older woman with a beaky red nose and a black shawl gathered around her thin person.

Fortuna glared and his right hand jerked up. Lucky jumped back.

But the girl laughed. "Thank you, I think."

Lucky saw Fortuna relax.

Huge paneled double doors loomed ahead, ready to swallow them.

Fortuna's hand dropped. "Alice, it grieves me to own that this is, indeed, my fool brother. But I promise he won't trouble or insult you *ever* again." His eyes cut through Lucky. "He won't so much as look in your direction."

"What's this?" said a tall man blocking the doorway. He glared at a pocket watch attached to a long chain which disappeared into his waistcoat, then peered at Lucky over a tiny pair of gold-rimmed spectacles. His pressed black suit said boss-man, and his pinched expression gave the impression that he smelled something foul.

"My brother, sir," Fortuna said.

"He's full of nasty talk about loose women," the old lady said.

The man, who Lucky realized must be the overseer, frowned deeply.

"Show me your hands," he demanded.

Lucky held them out.

"Dirty nails to go along with a filthy mouth. Fortuna, I've been more than generous with your people, but I'll not have the likes of this sea-born pollywog infecting my mill."

Lucky started to protest. Who did the great galoot think he was? He shut his mouth just in time and smiled. "Thank you, sir. I'll just be off—"

Fortuna grabbed Lucky by the collar. "I'm sorry, sir. The boy's an orphan and not had the benefit of a proper upbringing."

"What in the blue blazes?" Lucky turned on him.

"Silence." Fortuna slapped the back of his head and clamped a hand over his open mouth. Lucky struggled, but his head was in a vise.

"I promise you, Mr. Briscoe, if you take pity on the

wretch, I'll get him to change his lowborn ways. With the example of the good people here at the mill, he can't help but be reformed."

Mr. Briscoe peered again at Lucky, and then faced Fortuna. "One chance, Fortuna. That's all."

"You won't be sorry, sir."

Fortuna slipped his other hand under Lucky's arm and dragged him into the mill. He pulled him over to an empty corridor, away from the ears and eyes of the other workers.

"Keep your fool mouth shut," Fortuna whispered. "If you don't, I'll slit your throat. Only way you'll return to sea is as bait, understand?"

Lucky tried to nod but Fortuna's hand still held his face.

"I don't want to hear your voice again today."

Lucky blinked.

Fortuna relaxed his grip and turned back into the main hallway. Lucky shook off his hand and rubbed the back of his neck, his skin burning with humiliation. Fortuna pushed him back in line with the other workers and followed Lucky up a wide staircase. The stair treads vibrated under Lucky's feet. When he touched the long metal handrail, it felt warm and alive. Pulling his hand away, he glanced back down. A line of people snaked behind. Like a current, they carried him forward. With each step, the air became thicker. He sneezed, once, twice. Fortuna turned on him with a savage glare but by this time, they'd reached the third floor.

In an anteroom, Fortuna grabbed a pair of white overalls from a hook and held them up to Lucky.

"These'll do."

Lucky hesitated, but when Fortuna dropped them at his feet and started to pull on a pair himself, he relented. The worn, downy cloth reminded him of a sail. Instinctively, he turned to find the harbor. Like boxing a compass, on land a sailor got his bearings by his position relative to the sea. But the only window in the narrow room was too high to look out from.

It didn't matter, he told himself. He wouldn't be here long enough for it to matter.

His guardian sauntered to the opposite side of the room, where another door connected it to the main floor. Lucky quickly tucked Pa's kerchief into the neck of the overalls and followed.

Lucky was in the belly of the whale now. Fortuna said something, but it was drowned out by the dissonant thunder of machinery. The mill was alive with hundreds of large looms and thousands of spindles, contraptions so immense they covered the floor. He couldn't tell where the room ended because the air, though moist and warm, was full of snow.

It put him in mind of New Orleans last summer, when the *Nightbird* awaited repairs at port. He, Pa, and the second mate, Sturgis, had been made to stay aboard. "No need to borrow trouble," Cap'n had said. So they'd watched from the deck as a windstorm whipped up the Mississippi. Huge bales of cotton shifted, rolled, and slowly came apart. He and Pa had watched and laughed as the Queen of the South turned white as Christmas.

The memory tugged at the corners of his eyes. The same

30

bits of cotton filled the air here, but there was no benevolent wind to blow them away. Instead, they hung like a sinister cloud in the stifling hot room, making it hard to see, hard to breathe. Lucky sneezed. *Like walking in a dream*, he thought, and closed his eyes. He tried to wipe the fibers from his face. He pulled Pa's kerchief up over his mouth and nose. But there was no escaping them or the jarring clamor of the machines.

Fortuna yanked his sleeve and pulled Lucky behind him across the floor. As they passed appendages that spun and clicked, eyes appeared. Lucky realized there were people perched on stools in the midst of the spinning, and others rushing about to attend to the cylinders that were lined in rows along the tops of the machines.

"That's the one." The old woman from the line pointed a shaking finger at Lucky and said something to the woman sitting next to her. Lucky couldn't hear what she'd said, but from the look on the second woman's face, you'd have thought he'd paid for goods with a loose topsail.

Fortuna's eyes narrowed. "You've made a bad start to your work here. Already the old hens cluck about you."

"Start out as you mean to keep on," Lucky mumbled, repeating one of Pa's oft-told axioms.

Fortuna spun around. "Did you speak?"

Lucky shrugged and shook his head.

Fortuna led him across the floor, closer to the heart of the beast. Lucky resisted but it was no use. He couldn't think, couldn't act. He felt as if he'd been stung by a jellyfish and was being carried along by the current against his will.

At least there were windows. Through one of the openings, he finally caught a glimpse of the harbor through the motes and lint. He breathed a relieved sigh. It was still there, waiting for him. But Fortuna turned a corner, dragging him behind, and it was gone.

"This is Spinning Room Three," Fortuna announced, pushing a sliding door and holding it open to let Lucky pass.

The panel clanked back in place behind them.

Lucky gulped, gazing about the room in panic. It was as though he'd been pulled underwater without a breath. Standing still, he willed his heart to slow. First one small breath, then another. The heat was intense and moist, worse than the most mosquito-ridden ports amidst the jungles of South America. Sweat beaded on his neck and trickled down his back.

He took a step into the room and the floor beneath him moved. Lucky grabbed fistfuls of air as his feet flew out from under him. He landed hard on the floor.

"Look here, boys! Puny whaleman can't keep his balance on a greasy floor!" Fortuna pulled Lucky up by the collar.

For a few moments, laughter pierced the clicking roar of the spinning machines. Lucky straightened his back and tried to ignore the landlubbers' taunts. A group of men wearing the same white overalls lined the room, each occupying a stool in front of a long row of cylinders.

"Be surprised if that one's ever been around a whale," said a tall boy standing a few feet away. Red spots marred the boy's light brown face, and Lucky guessed he was about fifteen.

Regarding the boy for a moment, and deciding he could probably come out the winner in a skirmish, Lucky stepped forward. Fortuna had turned to speak with one of the other men. "You wanna get up from your sewing and see just what I can do, you fiddle-brained figurehead?" Lucky said in the boy's ear.

The spots faded as the boy's cheeks turned red. He started to stand, but Fortuna already had Lucky by the collar.

"Don't let the boy rile you, Gaspar," Fortuna said.

"I'd like a chance to put him in his place," the older boy said.

Lucky raised his eyebrows and smiled. *Like to see you try,* he thought.

Fortuna cuffed him. "You're in my territory now," he growled. "You best listen and learn. And keep your fool mouth shut."

"You tell him, Fortuna," one of the men called.

The boy glared at Lucky, his eyes slits.

Lucky's gaze followed the row of machines, regarding each spinner in turn. To a man, they glared back at him. Until he got to the very last one.

A boy with skin dark as a moonless night at the equator smiled at him. Lucky narrowed his eyes, immediately suspicious. *That landlubber wants something from me,* he thought, *sure as scurvy.*

Slip Knot

A half day making a fool of yourself in the spinning room ain't much of a workday," Fortuna said as the shift finished and men trickled onto the street. "Now go directly to Mrs. Cabral's and earn your keep."

"I need the gear in my duffle," Lucky replied. "If you tell me where it is, I'd be pleased to fetch it."

Fortuna only laughed and cuffed him on the back of the head.

Lucky watched as Fortuna and Antone, the cussed scalawag who'd played first mate in his shanghai, disappeared into one of the many taverns that lined South Water Street.

Then he turned on his heel and headed in the opposite direction of the boardinghouse, making his way down Union Street to the waterfront.

His nerves were wound tight as a spool of thread. Pressing the cords on the back of his neck, he moved his head from side to side and felt a pop. His ears rang with the absence of the constant roar of the engines and clacking of the spindles, and his chest hurt from breathing the lint-filled air. In all the whales he'd chased, dirty weather he'd sailed through, and dangerous ports he'd visited, Lucky couldn't remember a time when he'd been more tired.

For hours he had scampered across the mill's slippery floor, following Fortuna's barked orders. Cleaning, sweeping, fetching, and trying to stay out of the way of the doffers, whose job it was to remove the spinning frames once they filled with thread and replace them with empty ones.

And this had been only a half day. Tomorrow he was to report at seven bells!

He tried to shake off the dread, but it coiled around him.

The single bright spot in the day was almost a fight. Gaspar, the surly apprentice, had erupted into a tirade over a missing tuber, an instrument used to drop the cylinders onto the mule spindles. Ranting and raving, he had accused half the room, Lucky included, of stealing the device.

When the tuber appeared later under his own stool, Gaspar was sullen and unapologetic.

Only Lucky had seen the dark spinner recover the tuber from a bin of scrap threads and place it there. Their eyes had met. Lucky smiled, remembering.

He rounded the corner onto Bethel Street and considered going into the seamen's church for a moment to pay his respects to Pa's memorial marker. But Pa would have urged him to press on. The ship's agents would be gone soon, and another day would pass before Lucky could work on his escape. "Pull your socks up, Lucky," Pa'd have said. Lucky doffed his cap as he passed.

A long line of men snaked around the gray stone building on Taber's Wharf.

"Why such a crowd?" Lucky asked a boy with the smell of farm on his jacket.

The greenhand looked at him wide-eyed. "There's a new vein been found in California. They say there's gold to be had for the pickin'."

The door to Merrill's Ship Outfitters swung open and a small man stepped out and surveyed the line with a shake of his gray head. "If you're here to sign on in hopes of landing in San Francisco, shove off. None of Merrill's ships will be stopping anywhere in the vicinity."

Groans and heavy sighs rose from the crowd as the men in line wandered off in all directions.

"Heard they might be taking on crew at Hastings," the country boy said.

"I'll stay here, thanks." Lucky headed for the door.

"In case you didn't hear," the ship's agent said, not looking up from a ledger on the desk when the bell announced Lucky's arrival, "none of Merrill's—"

"Yes, sir, I heard. Gold's not what I'm after; unless you're speaking of the greasy kind."

The man looked up from his ledger. "You Black Jack's boy?"

"Yes, sir."

"Sorry to hear about your pa, son. He was quite a character. Be missed for sure."

"You knew him?"

"Only by reputation," the agent said.

Lucky laid a tentative hand on the counter. "Well, I'm just as fishy, sir, and furthermore aim to follow in his footsteps as a master rigger."

"Son, you could be the fishiest hand in all of Christendom, and no agent on the waterfront would take you on. Not and risk the wrath of the magistrates of this city, being as you…" He shuffled through a stack of papers on his desk. "have not yet attained the age of majority."

Lucky slumped against the counter. He'd been holding out a minnow's scale of hope that Fortuna had lied.

The agent handed him a small handbill.

Let all interested parties be advised:

Lucky Valera, a colored boy of Cape Verdean descent and approximately 5 feet tall, was born in May of 1838. Being under the age of majority, and without written permission from his guardian, Fernando Fortuna, is expressly prohibited and furthermore not allowed to ship out under the laws of the state of Massachusetts.

The lad has been cautioned against stopping at the wharves, pestering the good men of New Bedford. Any who find him at the waterfront are encouraged to box his ears and send him to M. Cabral's boardinghouse, Cannon Street. By Fernando Fortuna.

Lucky took a step back, placing the paper on the counter. His cheeks felt hot with shame and indignation.

"No need to trouble yerself," the agent said, the lines around his eyes creasing. "I'll not box yer ears."

"I thank you, sir." Lucky turned and left, the bell on the door jingling behind him.

What now? He peered down the street. Merrill's wasn't the only agent. Maybe he could find one who hadn't gotten the cussed notice.

No. More likely, he'd get an agent only too willing to mete out an ear boxing. Or worse. Men in the maritime trades had no patience for deception. Lucky thought about invoking whaleman's commandment #2 (lie, but never about anything important), but decided any agent worth his salt would consider protecting his ship from trouble with the law of considerable importance.

Fortuna had certainly shown himself to be the biggest toad in this puddle. Lucky gritted his teeth.

Aawk. The gull sailed low over his head, almost knocking his cap off again before heading south along Water Street.

Lucky brightened. "Ahoy, Delph."

The bird landed on a long wooden sign, which hung across the front of a building. Lucky hurried to catch up. The western horizon had taken on a rose-colored glow. He wondered if Mrs. Cabral had missed him yet. There were few people about. Likely, most had gone home for their evening meal. Lucky's mouth watered at the thought of delicious stew. But he had more important business to attend to.

The gull shrilled down at him impatiently.

"What in the blue blazes are you trying to—" Lucky gazed again at the sign above. "Rowland's Counting House," he read. He was proud of being able to read, though he'd resisted sorely at first when presented with the opportunity aboard the *Nightbird*, when the master's wife had offered to teach him. "Of course, you go," Pa'd said. "When someone throws you a line, grab it with both hands." Lucky glanced up and saw opportunity. Rowland was a name he knew.

He strode up to the door and twisted the knob. Locked. He put his hands around his eyes and peered through the window. Empty.

"Who dost thou seek?"

Lucky turned to find a girl in plain Quaker dress regarding him through wide green eyes. She was almost his height, with a shiny mass of hemp-colored curls that spilled out from under the edge of her black bonnet. She held a hatbox under her arm and a notice in her free hand.

When she smiled at him, his cheeks warmed and he felt a bit lightheaded.

She thrust the paper at Lucky.

"Good people of New Bedford," he read aloud. "The time has come for those with conscience to act. Come hear the words of Mr. Frederick Douglass, formerly enslaved in Virginia. He will tell you the harrowing account of his life in chains and how he escaped to walk among us a free man. Once you hear his story, you will be prompted to act as a person of conscience to end this abomination, which threatens to drown our nation under the weight of injustice. Thursday next at Liberty Hall."

She took a brush and jar of paste from the hatbox. Dipping the brush, she painted a place on the notice board.

"Hold this, please." She handed the glue to Lucky.

"What's it to me?" he said, torn between interest and an eagerness to be off.

"I'd have thought thee'd have a care about thy brethren," she said and turned back to the board, smoothing a copy of the meeting notice over the paste.

"But I'm no escaped slave."

"We're all children of the same Creator," she said, taking the jar of glue and turning back to the notice.

Lucky stared hard at her narrow back. "You talk like a book," he said.

She searched his face for a moment, then smiled. "A nice compliment, though I'm not sure you meant it as such. But I've read plenty."

"Do you know when Rowland's Counting House opens in the morning?"

"Have you important business?" she asked.

She mocked him, blasted girl! And she was littler and certainly no older than he.

"Very important." He puffed out his chest.

"I see." She raised her eyebrows. A small patch of freckles over the bridge of her nose lifted slightly.

"Captain Rowland owes me a debt." What possessed him to bother with this girl, he wondered? Still, he couldn't seem to stop himself.

"Owes thee?"

He nodded, biting down on his lower lip to stop his fool tongue from flapping. The walls of the counting house seemed to lean toward him accusingly.

"Godspeed collecting it. Captain Rowland has been at sea these thirteen months."

Lucky would have been angry, but as she spoke, the wind went right out of her sails. She suddenly looked so miserable that his irritation evaporated like morning fog.

"He's your pa, isn't he?"

"Yes," the girl said, the corners of her eyes creasing slightly. "I'm Emmeline Rowland."

The gull cried and they both squinted up at the sign.

"If that bird cries 'Nevermore', I'll be taking my leave."

"What's that supposed to mean?"

"Never mind," she said. "What does my father owe thee?"

"Well," Lucky tried to decide whether he should keep talking. "It's actually my father he owes," he admitted.

"What dost thou have to do with it?" She eyed him with suspicion.

"I'm here to collect." He felt his patience ebbing.

"Why didn't thy father come himself?"

"Dead," Lucky answered.

"I'm sorry," she said, touching a gold brooch at her neck. "I lost my mother." Emmeline pointed at the notice she'd put up. "She was devoted to the abolitionist cause. I intend to follow in her footsteps."

"My pa was the best rigger on the eastern seaboard. I'm gonna follow in his footsteps."

"That's a dangerous business."

Lucky's chin lifted. "I know my way around a ship. Once sailed through a hurricane off the Horn. Waves big as this building."

"Weren't thou afraid?"

"Nah, I'm so salty I float," he bragged.

Her eyes widened and the smile she favored him with stretched the freckles across her face. "Maybe there's something I could do for thee?"

He mustn't let himself get starry-eyed. If he didn't get out of New Bedford, the only steps he'd be following were Fortuna's. "Could you pay the debt in his stead? Aren't you in charge of the household, with your mother gone and your pa at sea?"

"He remarried," she said. "I have a new mother now. At least that's what she makes me call her." Her lips formed a thin and determined line.

"Does she beat you?"

"Worse." Emmeline tucked the notices under her arm and closed the box. "She sent me to Miss Patience Pritwell's School for Young Ladies of Quality."

"Doesn't sound so bad to me," Lucky offered.

"Thou hasn't met Miss Patience Pritwell."

"So run away," Lucky said. "That's what I'm doing." He gazed toward the harbor where fishing boats were returning with the day's catch.

"I have," she said. "In a manner of speaking, that is."

"You?" Lucky gazed at her with genuine admiration. Who'd have thought that so proper a girl could show so much gumption?

She said something in a low voice that Lucky couldn't hear.

"What?"

"I was asked to leave, if thou must know," she said.

He laughed out loud. "What could *you* have done?"

"Any number of things, I assure thee." She looked mildly offended. "As it happens, there was an unfortunate incident involving another of Miss Pritwell's students."

"*You* got into a scuffle? I hope you walloped her, and good!"

"I did no such thing," Emmeline said backing away as though to distance herself from the accusation. "We Quakers are peace-loving people."

"What happened?"

"The girl in question, and I shall not call her a lady, fell." Her eyes narrowed and her nostrils flared slightly. "It's my personal opinion that she tripped over her own silly feet."

"But you were blamed."

"I was a convenient scapegoat." She sniffed. "Betwixt thee, me, and the lamppost, I was only too glad to go." Her face brightened.

"What's so terrible about Miss Patience Pritwell's school?"

"What's so terrible about thine own life that thou'd ask repayment of a debt belonging to another?"

"A dirty-dog half brother who's appointed himself master and me slave."

"I wish I had a sister...or brother." Emmeline gazed wistfully toward the mastheads at the wharf.

"Not like Fortuna, you wouldn't! Besides, I'm a sailor and sailors are self-sufficient."

"No man is an island."

"I have to be. I was raised aboard a ship and don't have any friends here. And Fortuna's a dirtier dog than you're ever likely to meet. 'Specially up there on the hill with the rest of the codfish aristocracy."

Her lips pursed and Lucky wondered if he'd gone too far.

But after gazing at him for a long moment, she smiled.

"Perhaps we can help each other."

"How could I possibly help you?"

"Thou pointed out how...isolated I am. And besides, being male, thou can go places I cannot. I've a bargain in mind."

Lucky eyed her warily. "What kind of bargain?"

"Aid my cause and I'll aid thine. A caution first: it may prove dangerous."

Lucky expelled breath like an exasperated whale. "Danger's nothing to me. I once escaped a band of sword-wielding cutthroats in Madagascar."

"Then what I propose should be a cakewalk."

"How could you possibly help me? You already said you have no money."

"True. But the way I see it, money is not thy need. Thou needest a place on a whaling ship."

"You said your father is gone."

"True, but did I mention my mother's brother is also a shipmaster? Captain Abermarle Mayhew, of the *Perseverance*, which sails in two weeks time. A word in his ear from his favorite niece..."

"Never heard of him," Lucky said. "Does he sail out of New Bedford?"

"Boston. But he'll be stopping here to take on crew."

"I'm just looking to catch up with my ship."

"Thou may prefer Uncle's."

"Nah, the *Nightbird's* my home, the crew is my family."

"Please thyself, I'm sure Uncle would agree."

"There's another problem: I have no permission. Your uncle's not likely to risk trouble with the magistrates."

"Perhaps not, but did I mention he's devoted to the abolitionist cause? When I tell him thou has assisted me, he'll want to help thee. And as they say: blood is thicker than water."

"So I've heard."

The gull swooped off the sign and landed on the lamppost, tapping the glass with its yellow beak.

"What's thy friend's name?" Emmeline asked.

"Him?" Lucky pointed stupidly at the bird. What was it about this girl that made him so nervous? "I call him Delph."

She giggled behind her gloved hand. "Thou may be a skilled sailor, but thou hast clearly no knowledge of the science of ornithology."

"Orni-what?"

"The study of birds."

Lucky puffed his chest. "What do you know about it?"

"For one, that creature's a she-gull."

"I know it's a seagull, you daft landlubber. The songs of gulls were my lullabies as a baby."

"That's not what I said. It's a *she*. I think thy feathered friend is a girl."

Lucky stared at Emmeline for a moment, then peered back at the gull. Delph tap-tapped on the lamp globe again. "How can you tell?"

She smiled sweetly. "She's rather small for a male. Didst thou know, the gull isn't thine only friend about this eve?"

45

"What do you mean?" Lucky glanced around the street. Just a few clerks and banker-looking gentlemen about. A horse-drawn carriage passed and traveled down Front Street.

"A colored man. There, beside the candleworks." She pointed at the corner, but Lucky observed no one. "He's gone now." Shadows gathered in the doorways.

Lucky figured Fortuna must have finished his drink and come looking. But it wasn't like his guardian to slink away. Perhaps he was spying to see if the rich girl would give Lucky something he could steal. He looked for the gull, but it had vanished. A knot of dread settled in Lucky's belly. "I'd best be off," he said and started toward the wharves.

"What about our bargain?" Emmeline called.

"I'll take it," he said, turning.

"Fine. I'll see thee at the meeting."

Hugging the side of Hazzard's Ropewalk, he peered down the street toward the waterfront. No sign of anyone lurking in the shadows. Lucky advanced. The smell of whale oil and the sound of distant pounding made his feet feel lighter on the cobbles. Over the tops of the buildings, a forest of masts came into view. His breathing slowed, he was almost there.

But when he glanced back, he spotted movement in a doorway. A gull cried. Delph? He couldn't see a dark head in the gathering twilight, but the call seemed to urge him forward, toward the water.

He broke into a run.

Fisherman's Knot

Hurrying past the busy wharf directly before him,
Lucky made for the one beyond, a deserted-looking
expanse, grown grassy from lack of use.

He crept toward the water, where three wrecked ships in
varying states of neglect had been left to rot.

A bark and two brigantines rested side by side, hulls low
in the water. The bark was the oldest and most decrepit of
the fleet. Broken-off stubs were all that remained of her three
masts. She'd already sunk and listed to the starboard side,
her bobstays exposed like ribs with watermarks where the
tide had entered.

The gentle lap of the waves soothed his rattled nerves.
He ran a hand through his hair and bits of white fluff filled
the air around him. Lucky knew he should be hurrying to
the boardinghouse, but he needed to wash the stink and
grime of the mill off his skin and clear the lint from his nose.
All thoughts of pursuers and danger disappeared. Lucky
decided he'd take a swim.

Catching hold of a rope ladder, he boarded one of the
brigs. He climbed over the taffrail and crept toward the waist

of the upper deck. She was a sturdier craft, though her deck boards creaked in complaint under his feet. A lone white flag, fashioned from a bit of torn sail, flapped like bird's wings against the side of the hull.

Awk, awk. The gull flew over the top of his head and landed on one of the two masts.

"Hush, Delph or Delphine, whichever you are. You're not helping me with that racket."

The gull called again.

"Shhh," he pleaded. Hell's bells! How did one quiet a bird? "You'll have me found out and then I'll be in a barrel of trouble."

The gull peered down, lifting tail feathers in a way that gave him a suspicion, after what it had dropped on Fortuna. But it flew off again, landing aft, toward the stern of the ship, on the companionway staircase that led to the lower deck.

Lucky made toward the longest piece of mast. Once there, he took a quick look around and shimmied up.

Splinters bit into his sore palms, but at least he had a better view of the waterfront. If someone followed, he hoped to see before being seen.

Lucky surveyed the wharf and waterfront for as far as he could see. In the harbor, the fishing boats unloaded the day's catch. Nothing moved on the deserted shipping wharf. The air itself seemed becalmed, expectant.

The sunken bark below him would make a near perfect swimming platform. He clambered down the mast again and made his way to the port side of the brigantine, where its rail almost rubbed that of the bark.

Carefully, he lowered himself over the side of the brig and onto what was left of the sun-bleached deck of the wrecked boat. The deck slanted until it reached the water. There, the planks had grown waterlogged, leaving a platform he could swim from, sheltered from view of anyone at the waterfront.

He took off his shirt and tied it around a piece of the taffrail.

Lucky climbed down until he found a place where he could see the rocky bottom and the fish swimming below.

He dove into the bay. The silence underneath wrapped him like a blanket, soothing his nerves even as the salt stung his blistered hands. Opening his eyes underwater, Lucky wondered if the distant sirenlike sound was the echo of whales talking to each other, somewhere far out at sea.

He emerged into the soft light of evening and shook his head. A shadow moved on the water.

Lucky drew in a quick breath. It wasn't the gull. Someone stood on the deck of the brig, looking down at him.

He had to shield his eyes to see the figure outlined by the setting sun. The pounding of his chest slowed when he recognized the dark boy from the mill. His fear subsided, replaced by irritation.

"What're you doing here?" Lucky said.

"I wanted to thank you for what you did for me. I'm Daniel."

"Thank me?" Lucky swam over to the bark's deck and held onto the submerged rail. "For what?"

"Not telling on me when I replaced the tuber."

49

"Whalemen never tattle," Lucky said. "It's commandment #9."

Daniel looked puzzled. "Not in the Commandments I learned."

"Well it wouldn't be, would it? You're not a sailor."

"That may be, but I learned my Commandments, like all people who love the Lord."

"How'd you find me?" Lucky asked.

"Saw you aloft." Daniel pointed at the mast, then gave a shake of his head. "I don't like heights."

"Now that you're here, might as well come in. Water's fine." Why had he said that? Lucky needed to get back to the boardinghouse before he was missed. But the boy took a step back.

"Not me," Daniel said. "I hope to swim in the Hereafter, but in this life, I ain't able."

The boy's "I"s sounded more like "ah"s. "You sure talk funny," Lucky said. "Where'd you come from?"

"Alabama," Daniel answered, but more softly, and Lucky noticed his eyes dancing side to side when he spoke, as though he expected someone to challenge him.

"You got family here?"

Daniel climbed down the side of the bark, his movements slow and careful. He held tight to the side, as only someone afraid of the water would, and Lucky wondered if he'd be able to pull him up onto the deck if he fell in. Some no-swimmers couldn't be saved. They struggled so much that you couldn't let yourself get near 'em lest you be pulled under and drowned as well.

A dog barked and the boy trembled, looking around again. "I got no family here," he said, wrapping an arm around the taffrail. "I'm part of the Lord's family, of course, and I'm mighty grateful for that. But it'd be a powerful comfort to have a worldly family."

Lucky squinted up at him. "Don't be so sure. You know that bilge rat by the name of Fortuna? He claims to be my family. How's that for cold comfort?"

"True." Daniel smiled. "But perseverance in this life leads to reward in the Hereafter. That's when I hope to be reunited with my mama."

"I can't wait that long," Lucky slapped his hand against the water. "I won't have that scoundrel landlubber living off my labor. Not when I'm used to fending for myself. Is your mama dead?"

"I pray not. Master sold her a few weeks before I escaped. Wouldn't tell me where."

"You escaped slavery?" Lucky spit out the water that had collected in his open mouth.

"I did." Daniel stared back for a moment, then scanned the wharf.

"Is someone following you? You're not in league with Fortuna, are you?"

Daniel shook his head vehemently.

"You expecting someone?"

"Always. Man by the name of Jessup, overseer at my old master's place in Alabama and the meanest man in all of Dixie. Said if I tried to escape, he'd track me down. No matter how far I ran or how long it took." Daniel's Adam's apple jumped, and he licked his lips. "Every time I smell pipe tobacco, I wonder if he's come for me. Said he reckoned I was too afeared and too dumb to get far, but if I tried, he'd put me back into the chimneys."

"Why would he do that?"

"Before he put me in the mill, he tried to give me the job of chimney sweep. I told him I was afraid of heights but he wasn't hearing any of it; said he'd whoop me within an inch of my life if I didn't go up that ladder."

"So you went?"

Daniel nodded. "I went, all right. But once I got down in that chimney, I was too scared to come out."

"What happened?"

"Jessup blew pipe smoke up it 'til I was close to suffocating. When that didn't work, he lit a fire!"

"Did you come out then?"

"I did. But to this day, the smell of smoke makes my innards upset."

"How'd you go about escaping?" Lucky asked, skeptical that a boy afraid of heights, smoke, and water possessed the gumption to escape his own shadow.

Daniel settled more comfortably against the rail. "I like to tell folks my freedom was born of a promise. Once made, that vow could not be broken. Swept me along in the right direction. Promise, prayers, and the help of a lot of good people along the way."

"Who'd you promise?"

"My mama."

"Did you take up arms against your master and fight your way out of there?"

"No. I walked away."

"That's all?"

"It wasn't as easy as it sounds. I just walked at first, but then I had to hide in the woods. Small fella like me no good in the fields, so my master'd hired me out to the Magnolia Cotton Mill. That's where I learned to be a mulespinner. Anyway, I strolled out one night and just kept walking. Pack of dogs on my tail come morning, but I managed to stay a hair's breadth ahead. Across the fields, through the forest, out of Alabama, out of slavery."

Lucky studied Daniel. He suddenly felt lighter and more buoyant. As though Daniel's story had filled his lungs with a fresh gulp of air. "How'd you know where to go?"

"I followed the words of a song my mama used to sing."

> *When the sun comes back and the first quail calls,*
> *Follow the drinking gourd,*
> *For the old man is waiting for to carry you to freedom*
> *If you follow the drinking gourd.*
>
> *The riverbank makes a very good road,*
> *The dead trees show you the way.*
> *Left foot, peg foot, traveling on,*
> *Follow the drinking gourd.*

He sang the verses in a voice so clear and strong that Lucky could almost picture him running through fields and crossing streams, the cries of the hounds getting fainter as he fled, following the stars in that faraway night sky all the way to freedom.

"I know what the drinking gourd is," Lucky said. He drew the Big Dipper in the air. "Sailors use the stars to navigate, too."

Daniel nodded.

"My pa taught me to use a sextant before I was six years old."

"Your pa a sailor like you?"

"Was. See the rigging lines on that beauty?" Lucky pointed to a vessel on the neighboring wharf. All new and clean, just getting fitted out for her maiden voyage. He could smell the tar of her freshly caulked seams. "That's what my pa did. The standing rigging is the lines that support the masts, yards, and bowsprit." He lowered his hand toward the deck where a crisp expanse of canvas swayed in the evening breeze. "Running rigging is used to move the sails."

"Looks like a spider's web to me. How'd your pa keep from getting tangled?"

Lucky laughed. "He knew what he was about. Same as I do." He looked wistfully back at the ship. "Beautiful, isn't she? Take you anywhere you can think of. Round the Horn down to South America. You wouldn't believe the wonders you'd see; they got birds down there of every color in the rainbow."

"Sounds like you miss it."

"So much I can almost taste the salt horse."

"You eat horses?"

Lucky had to smile at the horrified look on Daniel's face. "It's what sailors call the awful beef the cook serves up at sea."

"And you like it?"

"Not exactly. But you get used to it."

"You'll get used to the mill, too. It's not so bad. I could help you."

Lucky stretched his arms over his head. "Don't intend to be around long enough to get used to it. I have to catch up with my ship. Besides, why'd you want to help me?"

"I could use a friend."

"You want nothing in return?" Lucky asked.

"You could teach me to swim."

"Why'd you want to do that?"

"Never know when it might come in handy, with all this sea around us. I'd sooner swim than sink."

Lucky considered the offer. It wasn't his practice to form bonds with landlubbers. But he liked Daniel, in spite of his jittery ways. Besides, anyone who could help him at the mill was helping him get around Fortuna. That couldn't hurt. "I have some escaping to do myself. But it may be a while before I get the particulars worked out. In the meantime, I could meet you here after the quitting whistle." He combed his hands through his hair and climbed up to retrieve his shirt and trousers.

"It's a deal."

"What rascally business are you two dark devils about?" a booming voice called from the deck of the brig below.

Lucky pulled on his shirt and trousers and prepared to run. Daniel was already over the rail and back onto the brig, but the man stood between him and the ladder.

"We meant no harm, sir. Just having a swim and a gam."

The man looked up at Lucky skeptically. "I had a swim meself, once. In the Pacific, somewhere off the coast of the Sandwich Islands. Look what it cost me!"

He stepped back from the ladder and Daniel gasped. Sticking out from the bottom of his short trousers, where his right leg and foot should have been, was a rounded piece of wood, which tapered off into a peg.

"Shark get your foot?" Lucky couldn't help asking.

"Whale," the man said, a note of pride in his voice. "Who's asking?"

"I'm Lucky Valera, sir. And this is Daniel."

"You Jack's boy?" The old sailor peered up at Lucky through red-rimmed, rheumy eyes.

"Yessir. You knew him?" Lucky stepped forward and started down the ladder. Daniel hung back for a moment then followed.

The gull flew low overhead. The sailor stumbled, nearly losing his balance. He took in vain two of the three names of the Holy Trinity. Daniel gasped. Lucky ignored him and stepped down onto the wharf.

"Delph! Stop that!"

The sailor shook his fist in the air. "Take more than a little birdie to knock old Raab off his peg!"

Lucky stood next to him and extended a hand. Though the sailor smelled of stale rum, he didn't seem too drunk. The gull flew off.

"You knew my pa?" he asked again.

"Not a sailor this side of the Atlantic who hasn't heard of Jack. How's he doing these days?"

"Gone, sir. I'm surprised you haven't heard."

Raab mopped his brow. "That's a shame, boy. Whaling is terrible dangerous business." He thumped his peg against the wharf. "'Tis a fact. This here's proof positive of that."

"Did you sail with my pa?" Lucky asked.

"Seems to me I did once." He pulled his stubbly chin hairs then wiped his eyes again. "I disremember the details, though."

Lucky sighed. "I understand, sir. Was he on the voyage when the creature did this to you?"

"Hmmm?" Raab followed Lucky's gaze down his leg. "No, boy, he was not."

"Did they kill the whale?" Daniel asked.

"Nope. And I can tell you, it's been a sore worry to me. That creature has chased me through more than one nightmare."

"Was he big?" Daniel asked.

"Big? You ain't seen nothing as big as that leviathan. All black and blowing his spout up to both sides. Clamped onto my leg with those giant teeth and like to have pulled me under and taken me straight to hell!"

Daniel stepped back. Lucky could tell he hadn't spent much time in the company of sailors. He wasn't used to the colorful talk. To Lucky it sounded like home. But he was having a hard time picturing Raab's leg in the whale's mouth. For one thing, the whale he was describing sounded like a right whale. Everyone knew right whales had baleen, not teeth. Must be a bit addled by the shock of the experience, he allowed.

"Can we do anything to help?" Lucky offered, looking about. It must be seven bells; he'd surely catch it when he returned to the boardinghouse.

"There's not many around here who'd throw old Raab a life raft if he were sinking. Let me think on that." He wiped his eyes again.

"We best get along," Daniel said and motioned to Lucky with a nod of his head.

"We'll be back," Lucky called as they headed up the wharf toward South Water Street.

"That Raab sure told some tall tales," Daniel said when they were out of range.

"What d'you mean?" Lucky glared at him.

Daniel opened his eyes wide and leaned in toward Lucky. "Do you think it could have been the drink?"

Lucky scowled. "What do you know about drink?"

"Only what my mama told me: never trust a man who drinks before supper."

"You don't know sailors," Lucky said.

"Speaking of knowing, I disbelieve that ole Raab ever knew your pa."

Lucky stopped dead in the street, the toe of his shoe knocking against a cobble. "Take that back," he said between his teeth, his low, threatening tone reminding him of Fortuna this morning.

"I'm sorry," Daniel said, looking truly remorseful. "It's just that when you been lied to a long time, you get mighty suspicious of what folks tell you. You also get pretty good at reading the signs that they're not telling truths." He held his hands up in the air. "I may be wrong. Hope I am. But I got the feeling he was telling tales because he wanted something."

"If that were the case, why didn't he ask? You heard me offer."

"I know." Daniel looked hard at him. "Let's just hope I'm wrong."

Lucky realized how late the hour had grown. He'd be in trouble at the boardinghouse for sure. "See you tomorrow," he said, leaving Daniel and running toward Cannon Street.

When he got near, he could see Mrs. Cabral coming down the front stairs. She sashayed across the yard in an elaborate dance, a rush broom waving in her hand. "There you are!" she called when she saw him. "You've left me shorthanded!"

Clinch

I'm sorry," Lucky said and he was. He didn't make the
bargain with Mrs. Cabral, but she'd been decent to him.
Besides, the ache in his gut reminded him of the fine
rations he'd had at her table.

"You've been at the wharves. I can smell it on you."

"Just went for a swim to wash up," he said, trying to look
innocent.

She lifted the broom and one-handedly swung it back
and forth over the already immaculate slate of the sidewalk.
"I'm no stranger to the ways of the sea. The sea took my husband and I've missed him sorely."

"I'm a powerful swimmer. Besides, Pa said I was born
with a caul. That means I can't drown."

"There are more ways than one to drown," she said, not
looking up from her sweeping.

"Yes, ma'am," he offered. Best not to question too
closely.

"There's some stew on the fire. After, I've some haulin'
and fetchin' needs doing."

"Thank you." He started up the stairs. "Mrs. Cabral?" He

turned to find her staring toward the wharves, broom still. "I'd be grateful if you didn't mention to Fortuna where I've been."

"No use borrowing trouble," she said. "Isn't that right, Beulah?"

Lucky hurried inside to the kitchen.

When he'd finished cleaning the fireplaces of ashes and stocking them with wood, fetching water, and pulling linens from the windowsills where they'd been set to air, Mrs. Cabral showed him to a small room on the second floor with a window that faced the back garden.

"This is a mighty nice room," Lucky looked around suspiciously. "Whose bed is the other?"

"I may have another boarder come in. For now, the room is yours alone."

"What's in here?" he asked, pointing to a wooden chest under the window.

Mrs. Cabral looked fondly at the trunk. "Some old gowns," she said. "Do you need a place for your clothes?"

"I don't have any. Fortuna took 'em."

"We'll have to see what we can do about that," she said.

Lucky eyed the landlady skeptically. Why would she offer him such fine quarters, and all to himself? And clothes? Sharing with a slew of bunkmates was how sailors were used to sleeping. Even in port, the Mariner's House packed men twelve to a room. Did she think he'd steal from the boarders? Maybe she wanted him to get up so early because she was afraid he'd disturb the others. That must be it. "What time do you want me to start in the morning?" he asked.

"Why don't you have a rest tomorrow?" At Lucky's surprised expression, she added, "Just this one time, mind you. And only because of that knock you took to the head."

Lucky narrowed his eyes. This was too easy. He didn't like the smell of it. But perhaps she wanted him to empty slop buckets, but was afraid the stench would make him fall on his head again if he started too soon. Best not tell her he was used to it, having been cabin boy on the *Nightbird*, he decided. Instead, he asked, "What kind of chores need doing in the morning?"

"Nothing too taxing. Fetch water and wood and coal, gather eggs, and start the fire."

He could stand it no longer. "Why are you being so nice to me?"

She looked at him for a long moment, lips pursed. She seemed to be between wind and water in deciding how to respond to his questions. Finally, she let out a sigh and looked down at her stump. "You're right, Beulah. The boy deserves to know." She reached out with her good arm and put her hand on Lucky's shoulder. "I promised your mother," she said.

The words hit Lucky like an arctic blast. Leaning against the wooden post of one of the beds, he tried to catch his breath.

"You knew my mother?"

"Knew you, too, when you were just a wee baby."

He stared at her. "How?"

"You lived here."

Lucky looked around the room with renewed interest. "Here?"

"Yes, this was your room. Though you were in a cradle."

"Why did we live with you?"

Mrs. Cabral studied the wall, as though the cracks in the whitewashed plaster were a chart of her memories. "Your pa was at sea. Your ma was a Kanaka married to a Cape Verdean. Her people didn't approve, so she came here. I liked her from the start. Wee slip of a girl. Fragile, like a tropical bird flown off course. But she had a strong and kind heart. Practical, too. Helped me through some hard times. 'Rosa,' she'd say, 'you may be short a hand, but you've twice the smarts of the other boardinghouse owners.'"

"Why'd she say that?" Lucky asked.

"Probably because I took her when no one else would." She laughed, but the corners of her mouth turned down as though the memory were bittersweet. "Weren't many women in this part of town back then. Most of the boardinghouses had only sailors and tradesmen from the docks."

"Why'd you take her?"

"There was something in the way she banged on my door. Holding you in a bundle in her arms, small bag at her feet. A fierceness that I felt akin to. Mayhap a part of myself I'd lost, mayhap a part I'd never had."

"Did you find it?" Lucky's head swam.

She continued as though she hadn't heard. "Your mother was special. She didn't like waste, see. In people or in goods. She saw that the back garden got planted and bartered with the butcher to exchange vegetables and eggs for meat. Made a deal with the milkman to trade for fish, offered to do the baker's wife's laundry in exchange for bread."

"Why'd she leave?" Afraid he already knew the answer, Lucky couldn't help asking.

"She took ill." Mrs. Cabral grasped her stump and drummed her fingers against the smooth skin. "I promised to look after you, but some of her people came and took you away. Later, I heard your pa'd convinced the wife of the *Nightbird*'s captain to take you on board as playmate for her son. I didn't think a ship was any place to raise a child. But at least you were with your pa."

"It was a fine place." Lucky sniffed. "The best." Still, part of him wondered what his life would be had his mother lived. He pushed the mutinous thought far away from his consciousness.

"I always hoped I'd be able to repay the kindness your ma showed me. Now I have that chance."

"You'll help me escape Fortuna?"

She shook her head slowly. "You've learned the life of a sailor. You like it fine, I can tell. But it's all you know. Now's your time to learn another life. See another way."

"I don't want another life!" Lucky cried. "Especially not one as a mill rat, slave to that bootlicking boss's boy!"

"I know Fernando can be a bit single-minded. So when I heard about him passing out those flyers down at the waterfront, I went to him. Told him I could use a hand running the place now that my former helper'd gone off to sea." Her smile reached all the way up her face, turning folds in the corners of her eyes. "I think your mama was right there with me when I made that bargain, don't you?"

"Fortuna means to get rich, no matter who he hurts."

"See, you've already learned something from him!"

"Learned what *not* to be!" Lucky felt even angrier when

she nodded at this, looking pleased.

"He also has the law on his side. Don't forget that. I'll see to it you're well-fed and well-treated here. It's up to you to do the rest. Make good use of your time; learn how to pull your weight at the mill."

"It's not fair," Lucky said, trying to swallow the whine in his voice. The hope he'd felt at having her on his side slid away like retreating surf. The combined weight of the past and present sat heavy on his shoulders and a to-the-bone weariness set in. He stepped to the window and opened it, stuck his head out, and took a deep breath of honeysuckle-scented air.

"You ill?" Mrs. Cabral asked.

"No, just tired."

"I'll leave you to rest," she said and backed out of the room, closing the door softly behind her.

Lucky wasn't sure he'd be able, but once he stretched out on the narrow bed, he felt himself falling deeper and deeper beneath the surface of sleep.

In his dreams he heard the mill's whistle, but from a long distance. He was back in his bunk in the fo'c'sle, the rock of a stormy sea letting him know that he was safe…

"Get up!" a harsh voice shouted in his ear.

Lucky fell off the bed onto the floor. He jumped to his feet, ready to fight. Looking wildly around the room, he tried to get his bearings. It came to him in a rush, like the whoosh of air as he ducked a slap to the head.

Fortuna gave the bed frame another push, his lip raised in a disgusted sneer. "Time to go."

Rolling Hitch

I thought the boy should sleep in this morning," Mrs.
Cabral said as she scrubbed the kitchen floor, her stump
hand holding the bucket still while she wrung the cleaning cloth. "There's food wrapped up by the door. Enough for
you, too, Fernando."

Fortuna grunted his thanks, grabbed the bundle, and
stepped outside. Lucky followed, not at all optimistic he'd
see his share.

"You'd better not be so lazy you lose your place with Mrs.
Cabral," Fortuna warned as they walked down the street. "I
couldn't believe my luck when she said she needed some
help. Got a handsome deal, too. If you foul it up, you'll be
a long time regretting it."

"I won't," Lucky said and kicked at a weed that grew
along the side of the street.

When Antone and some of the other mulespinners
appeared, Fortuna hurried ahead to meet them. He threw a
chunk of bread back and Lucky caught it eagerly.

Lucky took a big bite, happy to be rid of his guardian.

A moment later a loud squall let him know Delph was
about and keen to share his breakfast.

"Go get yourself a clam," he called to the hovering bird.

"Morning." Daniel appeared beside him.

"Where'd you come from?"

"I board over to Mr. Bush's, just there." Daniel pointed at a large shingled house on South Water. "He's one who takes in fugitives."

"There are others?" Lucky asked.

"Plenty. I'm more blessed than most, though, 'cause I got trained as a mulespinner back in Alabama. Here, it's a job wouldn't normally be open to someone like me. But I'm good at it. Once Mr. Briscoe saw what I could do, he hired me on the spot."

"Don't know how it could sit right with you, doing the same thing you did as a slave."

"It'd be wasteful for a man not to use the skills God has seen fit to give him."

"Do you sometimes feel like you're back in that mill in Alabama? Do you forget you're free?"

Daniel looked at him as though he'd just blown a spout of water from a hole in the top of his head. "Even the air tastes different to a free man."

They walked on awhile in silence.

"Tell you what does bother me," Daniel said.

"What's that?"

"Mills making fortunes on the backs of slaves."

"I thought I was the only one who didn't collect a wage. They pay you, don't they?" Lucky asked.

"Sure, they pay me. But where do you think those bales of cotton come from? Slaves! Do you know what happens to a back bent over day after day, year after year?" Daniel stood rigid. "It won't straighten anymore. When I heard about the trouble they had at the abolitionist meeting over in Lowell, I'd have liked to show 'em a few of those bent spines."

"What sort of trouble?" Lucky wanted to know. He wasn't looking forward to meeting Emmeline at the meeting tonight; best know what to expect.

"They threw stones at the abolitionists! Stones!" Daniel's voice rose in indignation.

"Where's Lowell?" Lucky thought he'd heard of it, but he didn't concern himself with landlubber places.

"A day north of here. Lots and lots of mills."

They'd closed some of the distance between Fortuna and the others, who looked back at them and jeered.

"They don't like me, 'cause I can spin faster and more than they can. I meant it when I said I'd help you learn the ropes." Daniel spread his arms, palms extended.

"*Era negro de quintal de nha pai,*" Antone said in a loud voice. The men around him laughed.

Lucky looked over at Daniel, hoping he didn't understand Portuguese. Antone had just said, "He's a slave on my father's plantation." But Daniel walked on, intent on the pattern of cobbles on the street.

"I don't let the others get under my skin. I'll meet my reward in the Hereafter," Daniel said, but when Lucky looked over, the line of Daniel's jaw showed his teeth were clenched.

"It's the herenow I'm interested in," Lucky replied, taking another mouthful of bread.

The gull swooped and stole a piece off the end of the loaf.

"Hell's bells!" Lucky shouted and then to Daniel said, "Best be careful what you wish for. What if your only reward is to come back a dratted, thieving gull?"

"I've often wondered what it'd be like to fly." Daniel sighed. "But I'm scared of heights."

They trudged on until they passed into the shadow of the building.

"When we get to the spinning room, just follow my lead," Daniel said as they joined the ranks of workers in line outside the door.

Fortuna appeared, grabbing Lucky by the shirt and pulling him off to the side. "Remember what I said about keeping your mouth shut," he warned. "And stay away from that colored boy."

"Why?"

"He's not one of us."

"He's not much darker than we are."

"He's not at all the same as us," Fortuna hissed. "We're Cape Verdean, he's colored." An ugly sneer raised the side of his mouth, and Lucky noticed that his teeth were almost as square as the factory windows.

"Hallo," someone called behind them. "Fernando, is that you?"

They turned to see Alice. Lucky looked to Fortuna, and as he watched, the ugly expression on his guardian's face transformed to pleasure, then longing, and finally steely determination. Fortuna slicked his hair back, harpooned Lucky with a don't-cross-me look, and strode over to where Alice waited.

Lucky hesitated for a moment, then turned to see the lady with the black shawl glaring at him.

"Morning, ma'am."

"I'm surprised to see you," she said. "Your type usually doesn't last a day."

"My type?"

She nodded. "Careless."

Lucky opened his mouth to make a comment about the nosy, complaining, sourpuss old-lady type but caught himself just in time. Instead, he smiled widely. "And miss seeing your smiling face? No, ma'am, not a chance!"

She looked away.

"Your brother is sweet on Miss Alice," Daniel observed.

"Only person that scoundrel cares about is himself," Lucky said.

"That may be, but I have a feeling all his scheming has something to do with her."

"What would she want with him?"

"Might be she wants him for a husband."

"What's he got to offer other than a bad temper and a greedy nature?"

"He's a man of some means," Daniel said as they stepped through the door, "especially now that he's collecting two wages."

In a dark mood, Lucky followed Daniel up the stairs to Spinning Room Three.

All that day, he watched and did as Daniel suggested. As loud as it was in the spinning room, Lucky was sure no one was able to pay much attention to anything other than the constant rotation of the big wheel, the rhythmic *click, click,*

click of the cylinders as they were filled with thread and replaced while the wheel still spun, marking the minutes and hours. But Fortuna's eyes followed him everywhere.

Lucky watched Daniel at work. His hands flew up to the cylinders, repairing the broken ends of thread before Lucky could even see they were broken. Sweat glistened on Daniel's brow. He wiped it with a forearm and kept moving up and down the lines, putting up the ends of thread and repairing snags. Doffers, whose job was to replace spinning frames with thread, also occupied the floor, crossing the spinners as they worked their way around the machines as though weaving a net of fine threads.

Lucky moved down the row, sweeping fluff and ends of thread out of the way of the spinners and doffers. It was impossible to keep up. His head swam with the effort, and he paused for a moment, leaning against his broom.

Just then a shout rang out, loud enough to be heard over the machines. And then a scream, even louder. Anxious looks passed among the spinners and soon the huge wheel squeaked to a stop.

The spinners remained at their stools, except for Antone, who rose at a nod from Fortuna and passed quickly through the sliding door toward the cry.

In a moment Antone reappeared, nodded to Fortuna, and spoke to the spinner nearest the door. Word spread down the line until it finally reached Lucky: a worker in Room Two had gotten an arm caught in the loom. By the time the machine could be shut down, her bones had already been crushed.

"Better take care, little nipper," Antone teased, "or you

could look just like your landlady." He pulled his arm into the body of his shirt, leaving the sleeve dangling. Parading across the floor, he swung the sleeve into the faces of the spinners. "Then Fortuna'd have a heap of trouble; what good is a one-armed sweeper?"

Little more was said amongst them, and soon the call came to make ready. Lucky worked his broom over to Daniel's machine, so that when the mill wheel resumed, he could watch.

"Does it happen often?" he whispered.

"About every two or three weeks," Daniel replied. "Briscoe tries to keep it quiet. Doesn't want the reformers reporting on conditions."

With a grinding whirr, the mill came back to life and again the spinners bent over their machines. Daniel pointed to the cylinders that needed threads put up. Lucky felt suddenly wary of getting too close. His right arm had begun to ache, and the furious twirling of the mules looked even more menacing. But after a while, he began to spot the barely perceptible thinning that would lead to a break. His friend's hands moved in a blur over the reels, down the rows, here and there adjusting a machine, repairing a snag. Lucky could see why the other mulespinners were jealous. Daniel did it all seemingly without effort, his feet never leaving the ground.

One could probably work a lifetime and not be as good. Lucky supposed it was a bit like being a master rigger. You either had it in you to work the heights and the tight puzzle of ropes and knots, or you didn't.

The heat and thick air of the mill bothered Lucky the most. He'd slept in many a stuffy and smoky fo'c'sle, but aboard ship one could always escape to the cool, fresh air of the deck. When they sailed into southern waters and the nights became hot, the crew often slept under the stars. Here in the mill, there was no escape from the heat. The air was so filled with lint it was hard to breathe, and many of the spinners and doffers who had been there as long as Antone coughed and wheezed their way through the shift. Lucky lifted Pa's kerchief over his nose and mouth.

Just two weeks, he thought as the hours crept past. A body could put up with anything for two weeks, he reminded himself as he slipped for the third time on the oily floor. And wasn't he more hardy than a dozen of these landlubbers? He looked around the room. They might work long hours, but whalemen worked around the clock, sometimes days at a time, with only a few hours' sleep. Why, they'd worked so hard last year when the *Nightbird* had run into a pod of greasy luck, he'd forgotten his own birthday.

Lucky sucked in a ragged breath. He reached up to loosen Pa's kerchief, hand shaking as his fingers fumbled with the damp cloth.

"Are you ill?" Alice stood beside him.

"What day is it?" he asked.

"Wednesday."

"The date, I mean."

She hesitated for a moment. "It's the third. What's the matter, Lucky?"

73

He'd done it again. He'd forgotten his birthday. As of yesterday, he was fourteen years old.

He opened his mouth to tell Alice, but stopped. Something about the concerned look on her face pulled at him, making his throat ache. He breathed in the oily smell of the spinning machines. "Just need some air," he said, and walked toward the stairwell. As the door closed with a hard clank behind him, Lucky grasped the railing.

But even with his eyes shut, he couldn't escape the presence of the mill around him. The vibration of its machines carried through the floors, up the rail, and into his fingers and bones.

"Are you sure you're all right?" Alice had followed him out onto the landing.

Lucky blinked hard. "Better not let Fortuna catch you here."

"Why? Fernando has no say over what I do. Besides, I think he'd want me to check on you."

How could he explain? He must warn Alice, for she clearly had the little end of the horn where Fortuna was concerned. He cleared his throat. "A caution about Fernando, ma'am."

She stepped back, looking puzzled, then held up a hand. "I know what you mean to say. He's gruff—hard even, I know. But surely not beyond hope."

Lucky eyed her skeptically. Was she truly addle-brained, or just having a go? But her hazel eyes were wide and her freckled brow wrinkled with concern. He felt strangely lonely now.

"I have a brother, back at home, just about your age," she said. "You remind me of him."

Lucky stood straight. "How old?"

"Fourteen."

He relaxed. "I'm glad it wasn't you got hurt earlier," he said.

Alice sighed deeply. "I know her. The one who got caught. Fine worker and a good girl."

"What happened?"

"Turned her attention away—just for a split second." She shook her head slowly. They stood in silence, and Lucky wondered what the future would bring for the injured woman.

"You've got to pay attention every moment," Alice said softly, "lest you end up with a life not of your choosing."

Lucky's cheeks burned. He thought back to the moment when he was snatched off the street by Fortuna. Was he here now because he'd failed to pay attention? Is that what she thought? He took a deep breath and tried to speak in a normal tone. "Are you saying you chose to work at the mill?"

She beamed at him. "I did. And my wages support my mother and the six little ones still at home."

Her words were more than he could take. The control he'd worked to gain sailed out the window and it was all he could do to keep his voice steady. "Well I *didn't* choose! Your sweetheart Fortuna chose for me! My wages go toward securing your future!"

Alice stepped back from the rail. She opened her mouth, then shut it, backing away from him like he had a pox.

She looked so hurt and bewildered that the anger drained from his temples down into his gut, where it sat like a lump of salt horse. She turned away, as if to collect herself before leaving the stairwell. He thought about what she'd said about Fortuna not being beyond hope. Unbidden, the memory of his last birthday came back to him.

Lucky had expected Pa to get him his first rigger's knife as a gift. But when the *Nightbird* docked in Vera Cruz, Pa'd gone out on one of his benders, arriving back on board with only moments to spare before they'd sailed. Lucky'd made the mistake of asking whether he'd bought anything in port.

The pale skin under Pa's stubbly cheeks and the smell of rum on his breath should have been answer enough. "Don't pester me when there's work to do," he'd said, and swatted at Lucky like he was no more than a troublesome fly.

Later, when Pa was himself again, he'd bribed the cook with a bit of tobacco and gotten an extra ration of plum duff which he presented to Lucky the day after his birthday.

"Son," he'd said. "I'm trying to do right by you. I believe there's hope for me yet."

Lucky let out a sigh. He'd gotten a rigger's knife not six months later. Inherited when Pa'd died.

"What's going on here?" The spinning room door swung open, and Briscoe stood before them.

"The boy felt ill, sir." Alice stepped up to meet Briscoe.

"Indeed!" Briscoe pushed the door open and shouted against the frantic spinning and clanking of the machines, "Fortuna!"

He turned back to them. "You better get back to your loom, missy. That is, if you plan to collect any wages."

"Yes, sir." Alice stood tall. "I'll walk him back—"

"The boy stays here!" Briscoe barked. "Get back to work while you still have a job!"

Alice nodded curtly at Briscoe, shot Lucky a look that he couldn't read, and passed through the door. In the clouded din beyond, Lucky could make out the eyes of the other workers on them.

"You're a lazy layabout," Briscoe snarled, "and the sorriest excuse for a mulespinner's assistant I've ever had the bad luck to come upon."

For the second time in the hour, Lucky cheeks burned. He'd like to see this no-account fat-cat landlubber go up against a whale. Probably scare the stuffing right out of him. How dare he say that Lucky was lazy!

Before he had a chance to reply, Fortuna was through the door, bobbing and nodding like a fool, trying to kiss up to that son of a sea cook.

"I'm sorry, Mr. Briscoe. It won't happen again. You have my word!"

"Your word doesn't seem to mean much these days. Try to do a charitable deed and look what misery comes of it! I ought to toss both of you out the door!"

Fortuna bowed his head, but Lucky could sense his anger. It rose off him like heat rose off the spinning jennies.

"As it happens, I'm down a worker. So I'm going to give you and this sorry baggage you've brought with you one more chance."

"Thank you, sir," Fortuna said. He grabbed Lucky by the ear and pulled him through the spinning room door.

"What'd you say to Alice? Antone said she looked upset."

"Nothing." Lucky's thoughts raced. What would Fortuna do when he found out what Lucky had said about him? He groaned aloud, glad for once to have his voice drowned out by the machines.

The Slippery Hitch

Lucky passed the rest of the day feeling afraid of what Fortuna would do to him and ashamed at the way Briscoe had berated him. He tried to stay out of Fortuna's way, but the man watched his every move, barking orders that Lucky jumped to follow, lest he get a kick or a pinch or both.

When the whistle finally blew, Lucky searched the backs of the retreating workers for Alice. Not seeing her, he kept sweeping, hoping Fortuna would forget him and head off to the tavern with the others. After a few more minutes, he crept back to the room with the cubbies to drop his overalls down the chute.

Fortuna was still there, talking with some of the other spinners. "I've got to get to Mrs. Cabral's," Lucky told him as he dashed out the door. When he reached the street, he remembered telling Daniel he'd meet him at the wharf for a swimming lesson. He didn't much feel like it, but figured it might cheer him up a bit.

Lucky arrived first. He looked for Raab but didn't see the old sailor and decided he'd best not draw any attention to himself by calling out.

Delph appeared, perched on the same broken mast, and watched as he readied for the lesson.

He'd teach Daniel the same way Daniel was teaching him, by showing, then letting him try. The sunken bark made a good platform. Though the deck boards were slick where the waves lapped against them, it was better than the shell-laden mud at the shoreline.

Lucky found an old piece of line and used a slipknot to attach it to the taffrail. He stretched the line across to the other side of the deck. This would give Daniel something to grasp to keep himself above water.

By the time Daniel appeared, looking nervously over the old ship's side, Lucky had already washed off the grime of the mill.

"Come on," he said. "First thing you need to do is shed your fear."

Daniel entered the water slowly but proved a good student. Soon Lucky had him dunking underwater and paddling the small distance between the rope and deck.

"You'll be a much better swimmer than I'll be a spinner," Lucky said as Daniel surfaced after swimming a few strokes underwater.

"That's 'cause I want to learn to swim," Daniel said. "You don't really want to learn to spin, do you?"

"Nope."

"It might help you with your rigging."

"How do you figure?"

"Well, what's rope?"

"What?"

"It's hemp," Daniel said, speaking slowly. "*Spun* hemp."

Lucky considered this for a moment. The shadows had lengthened and he guessed it must be near eight o'clock. "I've got to go back to the boardinghouse," he told Daniel.

"Tomorrow?" Daniel asked eagerly.

Lucky nodded. "I'll have you swimming clear across the harbor in two weeks time." Delph squawked with approval and lifted off.

When he returned to the boardinghouse, Lucky started his work. Still feeling relaxed from the swim, he hauled ashes and fetched wood and water before he even saw Mrs. Cabral.

"You've done a fine job, and quick. Two hands make light work," she said and winked, passing Lucky a bowl of fish stew.

For the next few days, he looked for but never found a chance to speak with Alice. Still, Fortuna had said nothing to him about their conversation. Daniel's swimming was much improved. Often Delph and Raab showed up to watch his progress. At the mill, Fortuna seemed preoccupied with his own business and, aside from the occasional shout or shove, left Lucky alone.

It was true as well that Lucky was becoming more famil-iar, though not by any means comfortable, at the mill. He'd seen some of the other spinners plug their ears with cotton lint to block out the jaw-clenching sound. He tried it and found that it helped. With the mill noises muted, and a sailor's chantey to sing while he swept, the time passed more quickly than before.

Wednesday dawned with a crimson light. Lucky awoke early and looked uneasily at the horizon. Red sky at morning boded ill. He tried to do most of the evening chores before the mill whistle blew.

Tonight he'd meet Emmeline again at the Abolitionist Society meeting. Had she been able to convince her uncle to take him as temporary crew? Lucky felt anxious about this Mayhew, a ship captain he'd never met, and never heard tell of except from Emmeline. Also, not knowing exactly what she wanted made him nervous. Why had he agreed to her bargain without knowing the precise terms?

He looked around the boardinghouse and wondered who'd help Mrs. Cabral when he was gone. He shook off the thought. She didn't really need much help, he told himself. The boardinghouse was practically empty what with so many ships having taken advantage of the warm spring weather to get well away from the mid-Atlantic before hurricane season blew in.

Still, he felt a twinge and glanced uneasily out at the sky.

The workday at the mill passed like a ship on a dead calm sea. Fortuna had yelled at him several times and even pinched his arm when Lucky had been reluctant to get too close to the spinning wheels. Lucky rubbed the sore spot and promised himself that some reckoning would be in the offing before he shipped. After the recent accident, it seemed to Lucky that the machines in the mill had taken on a sinister countenance. As though they were alive and might, at any moment, reach out and catch a body in their bone-crushing gears.

"I can't meet you at the wharf today," Daniel said as Lucky swept past his stool.

"You going to the meeting at Liberty Hall?"

"How'd you know about that?"

"Half the town's papered with the notices."

Daniel turned toward him. "You goin'?"

"Might. Got some business there."

Daniel turned from the spinning machine. "What business?" he called. The mulespinner beside him, one of Fortuna's friends, looked up.

"Shhh," Lucky nodded toward one of the filling cylinders. "End's about to break."

Daniel brightened and reached to repair it. Lucky bit the inside of his cheek. What would his friend say if he knew the above-board truth: that Lucky'd made a deal to help the abolitionist cause, but only to escape Fortuna and New Bedford?

"We'll sit together," Daniel was saying. "Only we should split up beforehand and meet there so Fortuna doesn't suspect."

When the whistle finally blew, Lucky tore off the white overalls and grabbed his boots. He ran down Purchase Street toward Liberty Hall. The meeting would have already started and he wanted to make sure he didn't miss Emmeline and news of her gam with the uncle who could be his salvation.

What in the blue blazes would she want him to do to help the abolitionist cause? What could he do? Probably paper the town in more of those notices like the ones she'd put up the other day. A fair price for his freedom, Lucky decided. He'd put up as many broadsides as Emmeline could carry.

He paused at the door to the hall where a new decree, still wet with glue, had been posted.

CAUTION!
Colored People of New Bedford, one and all,
You are hereby respectfully cautioned and advised
that by recent order of the
Mayor and Aldermen of Boston
Watchmen & Police Officers
Are Empowered to Act as
KIDNAPPERS
And
SLAVE CATCHERS
YE in New Bedford Are NOT SAFE
If you Value your Liberty and the
Welfare of the Fugitives Among You
Keep a Sharp Eye Out for KIDNAPPERS and
Have TOP EYE Open

Lucky re-read the heavy black words. Could this be true? Did it mean all the looking over his shoulder that Daniel did was justified? He'd teased Daniel about being afraid of his own shadow. Did the words on the notice mean Daniel had real reason to fear, or was someone just trying to stir up trouble?

Probably, he decided, it was just some abolitionist banter designed to get folks riled up. This kind of thing happened all the time shipboard. Some or another member of the crew would have words with the master or one of the officers, and soon rumors were flying. Many a mutiny started just this way. Pa had warned him to keep apart from rabble rousers and believe only what he saw with his own eyes. Well he hadn't seen any slave catchers. Lucky hoped there really was an uncle and a ship, 'cause he hadn't seen those either. Keeping his end of the bargain with Emmeline would be the extent of his involvement, he resolved. Come hell or high water.

He tried to go up the stairs to the meeting room on the second floor, but found the way blocked with people.

A Quaker man with a walking stick tapped the stair. "Let the boy pass, friends."

Lucky smiled and bobbed his head as he made his way through the crowd. Approaching the door, he squeezed between two stout women with wide skirts.

"Bless you," one said, smiling down at him.

"The people of New Bedford will protect you, brother," the other added and pressed a coin into his hand.

Lucky tried to give it back, but she was already too far behind. He was being shifted toward the front of the hall as though carried by a current. He put the coin in his pocket.

"Brothers and sisters, Mr. Douglass's speech has been cancelled in light of recent events in Boston. I'm here to ask for your help," said a tall colored man from the podium. A hush fell over the crowd. The man's hair was parted at the side and emerged from his head like a fin. From the cut of his jib, he appeared to be a gentleman. He sounded like a preacher, though, and held the crowd in rapt attention.

Lucky scanned the packed room for a familiar face, but didn't see Daniel. The crowd was an even mix of colored people and Quakers. *These must be all the escaped slaves in New Bedford,* Lucky thought. Then he spotted Emmeline on a row nearer the speaker. She leaned forward in her chair, her hands gripping its edges. Where was her uncle? Lucky examined the faces around her, but no likely candidate stood out.

"The Mayor of Boston has turned against the free colored citizens of Massachusetts," continued the speaker. "He and the Aldermen have forsaken their own in favor of those who would put us back in chains!"

This stirred a wave of anger and indignation.

"Scoundrel!" someone shouted.

The man at the podium held up his hands for silence.

"The Mayor claims he's doing his sworn duty and enforcing the laws of this country."

"What about his duty to God?" a man shouted.

"There have been threats that similar actions could be taken here."

"Let them Boston idlers try to dock that mischief on these shores! We'll send 'em swimming!" a man in the audience yelled. Lucky recognized him as a colored stevedore who'd worked for the ship's agent of the *Nightbird*.

The dark-dressed Quakers eyed each other nervously. A man in the front row stood and turned toward the crowd.

He held a black top hat in his hands and gripped the rim as he spoke.

"Brothers and sisters, we must take care to condone neither violence nor bloodshed on the streets of our fine city."

More rumbling passed through the crowd.

"We need a plan," the man at the podium said, "should agitators from the slave states bring their unholy quest to our streets."

"I have a plan!" the stevedore said, "We'll put them in shackles and march 'em back to blazes!"

A moment of shocked silence passed. Ladies in black fanned their faces and averted their eyes while men wiped starched handkerchiefs across their brows.

"My good man," the speaker said, holding his hands out to the stevedore, "while I can appreciate your conviction, caution must stride with valor."

Lucky looked toward Emmeline and she waved him forward.

"The City of Light shall cast a beacon to the rest of the world. We must call for, nay, *demand* freedom for all this nation's people."

The crowd stirred. What plan would the speaker propose? Lucky started toward Emmeline but the crowd was too thick.

"Fugitives should band together and stay on alert, ready to mobilize at a moment's notice. The rest of us shall remain vigilant and watchful." The man lowered his voice. "I have it on good authority that the kidnappers and slave catchers will try to pass unnoticed among us until they are ready to strike!" His arm shot out from his side like a cannon, point-ing at the back of the room.

A woman in the front gasped. Chairs creaked and scraped on the floorboards as the crowd turned to the back of the room. People shifted in their seats, eyeing each other suspiciously.

"And one of our own must lead the fugitives out of harm's way. One who knows the wharves and waterways of these parts. One who can sail a small craft under the cover of darkness."

"I'll do it!" the stevedore jumped to his feet, his arms waving wildly.

"My friend, you're needed on the docks," the speaker said kindly. "To enforce the peace, as it were, and to organize the dockworkers to sully the plans of any kidnappers who light on these shores."

Where was Daniel? Lucky wondered as he studied the crowd again, hoping to see his friend among the latecomers. On the other hand, maybe it was best Daniel not hear what the speaker had to say. Spooked as he became at the slightest hint of danger, all this talk of slave catchers would set Daniel awash in a sea of skittishness. Besides, Lucky felt sure it was just talk. No kidnapper worth his salt would bother with New Bedford. How would he be able to tell the fugitives from the Cape Verdeans? Lucky chuckled to himself at the idea of a slave catcher conducting interviews on Union Street.

"I need a volunteer," the speaker was saying as Lucky turned to make his way out of the room. He'd wait for

Emmeline outside. Maybe Daniel had been unable to pass through the crowd on the stairs.

"There's your volunteer!" A clear voice sang out.

Lucky turned in time to see Emmeline standing and pointing toward the back of the room. He looked from one side to the other, but saw only Quaker ladies. His mouth went dry. Dry as a piece of hard tack. Hell's bells! She'd gone and volunteered him!

"And does this brave young fugitive know his way around a boat?" the speaker asked.

Lucky opened his mouth to speak. "I'm not a fugitive," he tried to say, but the well-wishers swarmed around him, taking all the air.

"Sailed a ship around the Horn during a hurricane," Emmeline called.

Lucky tried again. "You've got the wrong man!" His voice came out as a rat's squeak. But by this time, the crowd was on its feet. "Whaleman's commandment #10," he muttered, "'Never volunteer'."

Tomfool Knot

Don't call me Ishmael."

"Why not? It sounds like an able sailor's name, and we can't go about calling you Lucky. Too many on the docks know it." Emmeline stood with her hands on her hips. "We wouldn't want anyone to box your ears, would we?"

Lucky scowled. How had she caught wind of that?

The sun hovered low on the western horizon. The meeting had ended, and the people who'd crowded Liberty Hall dispersed for their supper, leaving Purchase Street quiet.

"We've got to be careful," Emmeline said.

"Why are you whispering? There's no one about."

Emmeline glanced around. "We don't know that."

A vendor pushed a wooden cart piled with herring noisily up the street.

"Fish here," he called, "Fresh fish!"

"That bill of goods you sold me was anything but fresh," Lucky mumbled. "Smells like something you found washed up on the rocks."

"Thou promised to help!" Her bottom lip quivered and her eyes pleaded.

Lucky turned swiftly like a fish avoiding a net. "Do you know what trouble I'll be in with Fortuna if he hears his mill slave is to lead the fugitives?"

"Don't call thyself slave," she said in a low voice.

"Why not? That's what I am."

"Thou seem free enough to run about town every evening."

Lucky narrowed his eyes. "So dost *thou!*" Emmeline winced and he dropped his voice. "Just because I'm able to get around Fortuna now and again doesn't change the fact that I'm his slave. And that's what I'll stay until I can do your bidding and ship out with your uncle. Where *is* your uncle?"

Emmeline ignored the question. "You don't know what some of these souls have gone through, Lucky. Mr. Douglass was beaten and nearly killed. If he hadn't found a friend who gave him his sailor's protection papers, he might still be in captivity…or worse."

"Protection papers?" Lucky'd seen such papers. Sturgis had some, and guarded them carefully, making sure to carry them on his person whenever he left the *Nightbird*.

"Identifying him as a free sailor. He presented them to the conductor on the train out of Maryland." She stopped and gazed at him.

"Lucky!" Daniel called, striding toward them across the street.

Lucky winced. Why'd Daniel have to pick this moment to finally appear? Soon the lamplighters would be about.

"Who's your friend?"

"Works at the mill. Don't tell him—"

Daniel reached them. "Good evening, ma'am." He bowed to Emmeline.

"Where were you?" Lucky asked.

"Some of the spinners heard about the meeting and hid my clothes." His glance fell to Emmeline again and then rested on the cobbles.

She elbowed Lucky. "I'm afraid Lucky's forgotten his manners. My name is Emmeline."

"This here's Daniel," Lucky said. "There. Me and him need to be going." He took his friend's sleeve.

"Proud to meet you." Daniel bowed again.

"You missed an important meeting of the Abolitionist Society," Emmeline said.

"Are you a member?" asked Daniel.

"I am. A new notice has been posted. Hast thou seen it?"

Daniel shifted from one foot to the other. "I've not, but I'm sure Lucky will tell me about it."

"It's a hurricane in a grog bottle," Lucky mumbled.

"Thy gull friend doesn't seem to think so," Emmeline said.

Lucky studied the Liberty Hall sign, where Delph gazed down at him, head tilted quizzically.

Awwk, awwk, the gull called.

"Here, Delph." Daniel pulled something from his pocket. He threw it into the air and the gull spread its wings and descended, catching the morsel in its open beak.

"Daniel and I have business," Lucky said, turning toward the wharf.

"But we're not finished with *our* business," Emmeline said.

"Get the particulars and find me tomorrow evening at Mrs. Cabral's boardinghouse, 24 Cannon Street."

"My swimming lesson can wait," Daniel offered.

"Swimming lesson? Why, Lucky, I had no notion of the many talents thou possess." A covered carriage rumbled past and Emmeline's smile froze on her lips. She took a few steps back, as though the bulk of Liberty Hall might somehow shield her.

The carriage came to an abrupt halt.

A shriek rang out. "Get away from her!" A tall woman pushed aside the hand of the driver as he tried to help her out the door. Though the street was nearly empty, the few people about turned to stare. "Don't just stand there, you fool!" the woman screamed, slapping at the driver. "Save her!"

Daniel gazed at the woman in alarm. Lucky raised an eyebrow. He and Daniel were standing a respectable distance from Emmeline. Was the woman addled? Did it matter? Should they run before her driver could reach them?

Emmeline held out a steadying hand, but her face had gone white.

"M-m-mother," Emmeline said. "Why art thou here?"

"Stand back," the woman ordered, "Let Charles dispatch these ruffians."

The driver didn't look so inclined, but Lucky wasn't sure he wanted to take any chances.

The woman charging toward them could have been the rich younger sister of the mean lady from the mill. They had the same angular shoulders, long noses, and smelled-some-thing-nasty expressions.

Emmeline's eyes darted up and down the street. Following her gaze, Lucky wondered if she might run, but then realized she was doing some quick figuring. She touched the brooch at her throat and seemed to collect herself. "These are my friends, mother." She stepped forward to shield Lucky and Daniel from the driver.

"Friends?" Mrs. Rowland shrilled. "A young lady has friends who are her own age and gender. You *said* you were going to the Ladies Sewing Circle. Imagine my embarrassment when I decided to surprise you and was informed that you were not, nor had you ever been, a member."

Emmeline lowered her eyes. "I can explain."

"I doubt it."

Lucky stepped up, ready to speak on Emmeline's behalf. The woman scowled at him.

"If you must know, *Mother*, I was attending the Abolitionist Society meeting."

"You went against my explicit instructions to stay out of politics!"

"It's not politics, Mother. We each need to take a stand for what is right. If father were here—"

"Your father is not here! And I shouldn't have to remind you of the promise you made to him."

"I've tried to obey thee."

"It's only proper for a child to follow the rules given her by her parents. You've never bothered to try."

"What about the rules given by God?" Emmeline said,

her body rigid. Spots of red appeared high on her cheek-bones.

"What an unnatural child you are. And what a disappointment to me and to your father. It may be a blessing that your own poor mother passed away giving you life."

Lucky saw Emmeline falter. "I've tried to do as thou asked, Mother," she said in a small voice. "I just wanted to help."

"You can help by knowing your place. Your father will be so distressed. First the debacle at Miss Pritwell's and now this."

"Please, Mother. Don't tell him about Miss Pritwell's." Emmeline sounded close to tears. Lucky glared at the cruel stepmother. Why'd she have to pile on the agony? Anyone could see Emmeline felt bad about what'd happened.

"There's nothing you can do here. These people have to solve their own problems."

Lucky and Daniel exchanged glances.

"Come now." The woman took Emmeline's hand and forced her toward the carriage.

Lucky's cheeks burned, the memory of Fortuna shaming him at the mill still too fresh. But as he watched, Emmeline turned back toward him. "Tomorrow," her lips said without making a sound.

The driver helped Emmeline and her stepmother into the carriage before climbing to his own seat. With a whistle to the horses, they were off, rattling up the street.

"Sad that her mama can't appreciate the goodness in that girl's heart," Daniel said.

"Tea party's over," Lucky replied, watching the carriage disappear. "If you want to learn to swim, we best get to the water."

They started walking toward the dock.

"I want to know what happened at that meeting," Daniel said, "and what business you and Miss Emmeline were talking about."

"There's trouble in Boston, is all. I'm sure it won't come here but they've been gathering up some of the fugitives."

"Gathering? Who's gathering?"

Lucky stared at the ground. "They called them 'kidnappers' and 'slave catchers,' but I don't see that happening here in New Bedford."

They trudged on in silence for a few blocks.

"Always figured this day would come," Daniel said and let out a deep breath.

"Folks here in New Bedford won't put up with those Boston shenanigans."

"It's not shenanigans. It's the law."

"Well, then, it's a law many will break in a brace of shakes. The constables around here will give no quarter to any kidnappers."

Daniel smiled absently. "Mayhap. But not everyone feels that way."

"Who doesn't?"

"Your brother and the other spinners, to start. They'd be glad to have me gone."

"They don't get to decide. Besides, where would you go?"

"Don't know. Canada, mayhap." Daniel checked the street on both sides and behind them.

"You don't truly think Jessup's out there lurking in the shadows, do ya?" Lucky said.

Daniel's voice was a hoarse whisper. "Don't know what to think."

"Fiddle-brained nonsense. We can fend off any no-account kidnappers who come along. You're not going to have to go anywhere. Nothing will happen. D'ya hear me?"

Daniel nodded, but the creases in his brow remained. "You said you'd teach me how to float," was all he said as they walked the rest of the way down Union Street toward the deserted wharf.

From all appearances, Raab had been long at the bottle before Lucky and Daniel arrived.

"Rum," Daniel said, and pointed at shards of greenish glass that littered the ground next to the bark's bow.

"It looks like he decided to christen it," Lucky said.

Farther down the grassy planks, Raab sat on a barrel propped against a tackle shack, which listed away from the water as though a wave had nearly knocked it over.

"Cussed Cape Verdeans," he shouted at the decaying ships. "It was you and all the rest of them damn foreigners cost decent American-born sailors their rightful place before the mast." He skimmed a shell into the bay. It skipped once then sank. "I'd a been a first mate by thirty if not for those dark devils. Sayin' I was a Jonah and that I'd scuppered the *Independence*." He let out a stream of spit. It arched like a rainbow and landed with a plop in the water. "It was all over for the American sailor soon as those Injuns from Cuttyhunk started shipping out, and that's the truth."

Lucky gritted his teeth at the barrage of ugly words.

"And here's to you, Cap'n Seabury." Raab rose unsteadily to his feet and relieved himself into the harbor. "For spreading muck about 'dereliction of duty.'" His voice grew high and nasal. "Losing that whale was a cock-up not of my doing."

He stumbled and, for a moment, seemed about to fall in. Daniel stepped forward, stopping when Raab lurched back.

"But who bore the blame? Me! Well, I showed that bloody greenhand what was what, didn't I? Who'd have guessed the bugger had a knife." He rubbed at his stump and an expression of intense pain clouded his mottled face.

Raab paced the wharf beside the shack. His head bobbed and jerked as though he were carrying on a conversation with a ghost.

"I was just going to rough him up a bit. No harm in that. But he left me no choice!"

He bent to clutch his peg. Falling over, he pulled at it, cursing as he did battle with the false limb. Finally, his stump came loose from the straps that held it on his body.

Lucky took a step forward but Daniel touched his arm. "Wait."

Raab maneuvered himself against the shed wall and addressed the black water.

"He died, 'tis true. But he was the winner of that fight, wasn't he? His pain was over but mine would last and last. You should have let me die that day, Lord." Raab let out a cracked sob. "'Stead of taking my leg."

Lucky drew in a breath. Daniel put a finger to his lips.

"I hereby commend thee to the devil and the deep blue sea," Raab called and tossed the peg into the harbor. It sailed through the air like a harpoon, then landed with a splash.

Lucky and Daniel stood in silence for a moment.

Finally, Lucky shook his head. "That rum-soaked, lying sot. It wasn't a whale what bit off his leg. He lost the limb after a knife fight."

"You're surprised?" Daniel asked.

Lucky thought about it for a moment, rubbing at the greasy residue on the back of his neck. He had to allow that he'd been caught off-guard by Raab's tale. Though, looking backwards, the signs were all there. The old sailor was no truth-teller. He based his story on what he believed the listener wanted to hear. And after the foul talk about Cape Verdeans, Lucky further doubted Raab had ever known Pa. Even if they had met, they wouldn't have been friends. Pa may have had his faults, but he didn't keep with blaming one's troubles on others.

They crept into the shadow of the shack where Raab lay, his naked stump at an awkward angle. Daniel found the old sailor's pea coat and dropped it over him like a blanket.

"I'll get his peg." Lucky sighed, and climbed down the wooden ladder into the water.

Twists

Delph dove at Lucky as he made his way down South Water Street.

"Stop fooling," Lucky yelled up at him. "I've work to do."

But the gull did not let up. She flitted up and down, darting and pecking at Lucky's cap. Finally, he settled on a ship chandlery sign, and let out a long line of cries.

Lucky gazed up at the bird. "Have you lost your senses?"

Delph shifted from one foot to the other. Lucky shook his head and, catching his own reflection in the shop window, turned to look.

His breath caught.

There, in the middle of a display of sextants, chronometers, and compasses, sat Pa's rigger's knife.

He gazed at it in disbelief.

It was Pa's knife, all right. He could see the finely etched rendering of the *Nightbird*, her bowsprit riding far above the surf.

That dirty dog Fortuna. He'd gone and sold the contents of Lucky's duffle.

He stepped into the shop.

"Where'd the rigger's knife in the window come from?" he asked the bespectacled shopkeeper.

"Just came in today," he said.

"Was it a tall dark fella who sold it?"

"That's the one." The man glanced up from his ledger. "Would you like to purchase it?"

"Purchase? It's mine!"

"Not unless you can pay. And I don't offer credit, young man."

"I'll be back," Lucky said and left the shop. A cold fury rose from his gut like Arctic dark. He'd find that no-account, thieving bootlicker and make him pay.

His fury gave him speed. In no time he was at the tavern where the mulespinners usually stopped on their way home from the mill. Sure enough, Fortuna was inside, his tiny teeth showing as he laughed at something Antone said.

Lucky pushed past the others to stand before him.

"You sold my things," he practically spat. "You had no right!"

Fortuna appeared bored.

"I'm your guardian," he said. "I've every right."

Lucky glared at him.

"You see what I was telling you?" Fortuna said to Antone. "Hey, half-pint," he said, grabbing Lucky by the collar. "The boys and I were just talking about the sorry behavior of the youths of this city. And your name came up."

Lucky eyed him warily. He'd been drinking, that was sure. He could smell it on his breath and hear it in his words, which had gone all fuzzy at the edges.

He should have waited for his anger to cool before confronting Fortuna. Lucky's gut tensed. He didn't have anything against drinking, as a matter of course. Whaleman's commandment #7 was "drink as much as you can hold." The problem was, as he knew well enough from life with Pa, the Valeras couldn't hold much. Not without getting dangerous.

"I've got chores to do for Mrs. Cabral," Lucky said and tried to shake free of Fortuna's grip.

"They'll keep, this won't. Let's discuss this outside." Fortuna leered toward his friends for encouragement as he pushed Lucky out the tavern door.

"Gaspar, here, says he should've whupped you for the sass you gave him at the mill. Said you could use taking down a few pegs and he'd like to be the one to do the deed." He checked behind him but the boy was nowhere to be seen. "Gaspar, come face your opponent."

A group of sailors leaning against the tavern wall laughed. Lucky searched their faces, hoping he'd see one of his shipmates, but it was no use. The *Nightbird* would be almost to the Azores by now.

In a moment, Gaspar pushed out of the crowd and staggered forward, a maniacal grin on his face.

"Leave it to me, Fortuna," he said. "He won't give you any more trouble after today."

"You're not to maim him too severely," Fortuna admonished. "Remember, he's in my employ and I'll want those wages." He pulled Lucky forward and pointed to his head. "No going for the eyes, hands, or legs, understand?"

Gaspar nodded.

"I need him to be able to sweep and pick up thread, see?"

"I won't hurt him too bad, Fortuna. Just teach him a lesson," Gaspar took another step forward.

Lucky bristled and shook free of Fortuna's grip. "It's you who'll be getting the schooling, landlubber."

"Listen to me, lads, the boy's been before the mast," one of the sailors called to his companions. "My money's on the sailor."

"Mine, too."

Lucky eyed Gaspar speculatively. He had the advantage of temperance, for one. Gaspar wore his condition on his spotted face and in his boastful swagger. He was like Mrs. Cabral's rooster. And like the rooster, he could catch a man unawares. Lucky mustn't let that happen. He already knew Gaspar had a mean streak; chances were he didn't fight fair, either.

"You're wasting your money betting against a mulespinner," Fortuna said.

"Let's see yours, you pasty-faced pieceworker," one of the sailors called.

Gaspar started toward him and Lucky moved to the side. They circled each other, dredging up the dust of the tavern yard. Lucky was sure the mulespinner'd try to get in a few cheap shots and finish him off quickly. But he'd probably not have the endurance or balance to carry on for very long.

"Let me show you how fast a spinner can move," Gaspar said and lunged.

Lucky jumped to the side, easily dodging the blow.

"I'll teach you to show some respect." Gaspar came at him again, sending a wild punch whizzing by his right temple.

"Not that way, you won't." Lucky laughed, though his voice sounded, at least to him, less than sure.

"No use trying to get the jump on a lad who rides the waves," one of the sailors taunted, while the others cheered.

Lucky stole a quick glance at Fortuna. His face was unreadable. A grim mask.

"Oh yeah?" Gaspar said and lunged again, this time catching Lucky by a shirttail. He pulled it hard and spun Lucky around, delivering a blow to the ribs with his elbow.

Lucky felt the wind knocked out of him. He tried not to panic as he doubled over, trying to breathe. Gaspar danced around him, slapping at his head. Lucky drew up quickly and knocked his opponent in the chin.

Gaspar winced, trying to smile. "Seems you've been in some fights," he said. "Too bad they were with little girls."

He charged again but Lucky dodged easily. *The mulespinner must be feeling the effects of the drink*, Lucky thought. His red face showed not only his anger, but also the direction of his next attack. Lucky could read it in his glance.

"You're the one who fights like a girl, pieceworker," one of the sailors called.

"You wharf rats better keep your blowholes shut," Antone said, and coughed into his hand. "'Less you want to fight, too."

The insults and threats flew back and forth like sharks circling a whale's carcass. Lucky tried not to pay any heed to the banter, focusing instead on his opponent.

When Gaspar tried to get in a blow to his side, Lucky jumped, extending his foot.

The older boy tripped and fell to the street.

"Huzzah!" the sailors called.

Gaspar jumped to his feet, charging blindly.

Lucky was ready with a fake to the right and a fist to the nose.

The bloodied Gaspar glared at him with the wild eyes of a wounded animal. He came at Lucky again. Lucky ducked and dodged. Gaspar lost his balance and fell to the street.

"The spinner's in his cups," one of the sailors cheered.

"Fin out," another taunted, as Lucky took a deep breath and nodded toward his supporters.

Antone stepped forward, shaking his head, but the fallen boy waved him away.

The white flash of a gull's wing near Gaspar's head brought Lucky's attention back to his opponent. Just in time, he saw Gaspar reach down with a sweeping motion and draw a knife from a holder at his ankle.

Delph cried out, as if in protest.

Another voice called, "That's not fair, pox-face."

Lucky had no knife. Whaleman's commandment #5 came into his head like a flash of summer lightning: "cheat before you get cheated." Well, Gaspar'd already cheated, he reckoned. He'd just even the score. Lucky remembered a stratagem he'd seen employed in a street fight in Manila.

"All right, you've won," he conceded. "I've no weapon."

The sailors' protests filled the street as Lucky moved toward Gaspar, hand out, as though to shake.

Gaspar appeared at a loss. Dazed, drunken, and stupid.

While he gaped at Lucky's extended right hand, wondering what to do, Lucky reached out with his left, seizing his opponent's wrist. He came in hard with his right elbow, catching Gaspar square on the Adam's apple. The knife clattered to the cobbles, and Lucky scrambled for it. Gaspar could only stand there, gasping for breath, as Lucky jumped to his feet, weapon in hand.

"Hurray!" the sailors cheered.

Gaspar favored Lucky with a nod of grudging respect before turning, shamefaced, toward his friends, who would not meet his eye.

Lucky felt the heavy weight in his hand. The knife, though not like Pa's, was substantial and well-crafted. But it wasn't a rigger's knife. Turning its handle so the sharp edge pointed toward him, he threw it at the wall of the tavern. The blade slid neatly into the weathered plank siding and stuck.

"Aye, mates, from his spout, ye shall know him," one of the sailors cried. "That one's a true right whale."

The sailors and spinners joined to exchange coin, each protesting the dirty dealings of the other. Lucky scanned the street for Fortuna, but he'd slipped away.

He stood for a moment, feeling suddenly unsteady. Not sure he could trust his legs to carry him.

Awk, awk, awk, Delph called from his perch on the tavern's roof. Lucky nodded up at him in thanks, turned, and started down South Water Street.

"Wait," a voice cried behind him. One of the sailors strode toward him with a gait that betrayed him as being newly aground. "The lads want you to have a share."

He dropped some coins into Lucky's hand, winked, and headed back to his friends. "Hope to ship with you some-day," he said over his shoulder.

Lucky checked to see if the mulespinners had witnessed the exchange but they had already headed into the tavern for another drink. He counted the money.

He turned back to the shops of South Water Street, walking quickly at first, then breaking into a run.

But when he arrived at the Ship Chandler's window, there was an empty space where Pa's knife had been. A "closed" sign hung on the door but Lucky could see movement inside. He rapped on the glass. In a moment, the shopkeeper peered out at him, pointing to the sign.

"Please," Lucky begged. "It's important."

The man glanced heavenward and unlatched the door. "I'll be late for my evening meal," he said. "Be quick, boy."

"I was in earlier," Lucky said. "Remember?"

"I remember. The rigger's knife."

"Have you sold it?"

The shopkeeper squinted down at him over the rims of his gold spectacles. "Why do you want to know?"

Lucky held out the handful of coins. "I want to buy it."

Taking a calculating glance at the coins, the shopkeeper smiled jovially. "Why didn't you say so?"

He placed the knife on the counter.

"Its handle is very finely worked," he said. "I don't think the fellow who brought it in appreciated such first-rate craftsmanship."

"I do," Lucky said, putting his money on the counter.

"Good," the shopkeeper started to separate the coins, "because you're a bit short of my asking price."

Lucky's breath caught.

"But I'd like to see it go to someone who knows quality." He tapped a long finger against his lip. "And I have a feeling you'll put it to good use."

"I'm grateful to you, sir."

"Want me to wrap it?"

"No need," Lucky said. He rubbed his fingers reverently over the ivory handle, then stuck the knife in the back of his breeches, the way riggers did.

The shopkeeper opened the door. "Hope you don't run into the former owner," he said, letting Lucky out onto the street. "I didn't much like the looks of him."

Shroud Knot

L ucky felt better the next day. No red sky greeted him
as he rose to the shrill order of the mill's whistle. He
rubbed the scrimshawed handle of Pa's knife and
returned it to its hiding place behind the bedpost. Last
night's warnings about slave catchers and kidnappers had
receded like land off stern. Just a barrel of stinky fish, he
decided. Fancy talk. Notions dreamed up by a bunch of
straitlaced abolitionists with too much leisure time.

Well, Lucky wasn't going to sail in that current. No, sir.
He'd be seeing the last of New Bedford soon.

He finished the morning chores and headed to the mill,
making sure that he left early so he wouldn't have to endure
the taunts of Fortuna and his worthless band of fiddle-
brained flotsam.

Daniel was at his stool when Lucky arrived. His eyes were
bleary as he bent to fix a spindle on his machine. Lucky wondered if he'd gotten any sleep.

"Are you all right?" he whispered as he pushed the
broom past where Daniel sat.

"Hmm?" Daniel looked up, startled.

Lucky could see the worry lines etched into his friend's brow. Blast those abolitionists and their scare tactics.

And blast Fortuna. As the day wore on, Fortuna became more and more irritable. Briscoe had warned him that a delegation of investors would tour the mill and all had better be in top order. Lucky could do nothing right. First, Fortuna was missing his oil can and blamed Lucky for losing it. Then, when it turned out Antone had borrowed it, Lucky was at fault for not knowing where it had gone. And when Fortuna stubbed his toe on one of the machines, it was because Lucky hadn't swept the floor thoroughly.

Finally, after Fortuna had pulled his ear for sassing back about the floor, Lucky was called into Spinning Room Two. He went gratefully, eager to get out of Fortuna's reach and put the bigger part of the day behind him.

Once you got used to the heat, it was just barely tolerable. The noise was the hard thing. Lucky figured he'd probably hear the whir of spindles and the pounding of the mules in nightmares for the rest of his life. He stuffed the cotton wool Daniel had given him into his ears and set about sweeping a patch of floor between two rows of looms.

The old woman, his nemesis, peered up from her work and scowled. He nodded and smiled at her. *I'm not going to let you ruin my day, you vinegar-drinking, prune-faced old biddie,* he thought as he swept. Even his feet felt lighter on the oily floorboards.

Wouldn't be long now. How many more times would he awaken to the whistle, he wondered. Twelve, thirteen? He did a quick calculation of the days until Emmeline's uncle's boat would sail. Worries about Daniel interrupted his thoughts. What if it were true that bounty hunters were coming? Either way, it bothered him to think of Daniel here alone, without a friend, after he left. Lucky shook off the thought. He couldn't worry about it. Soon he'd be back at sea, heading out toward parts unknown. He smiled and closed his eyes for a moment. He could almost feel the wind in his face, taste the salt on his lips.

A chantey, sung by sailors to make work pass more quickly, came into his head. He sang it softly, first to himself, then a bit louder. The spinning of the giant wheel blocked the sound, and none of the ladies even glanced up. Lucky squinted and imagined he was back aboard the *Nightbird*, swabbing her decks. The strokes of the broom beat a rhythmic tattoo across the floor.

Ol' Jolly Salts have sorry faults
Concealed beneath their britches.
They bring disease from overseas
Those scurvy sons-of—

A rough hand grabbed him by the arm and the broom dropped to the floor. He spun around, expecting to see Fortuna. Instead, Mr. Briscoe stood over him, lips white and jaw clenched. A line of three men in high silk hats and long-tailed coats stood behind him. One coughed uncomfortably.

It was only then that Lucky took in the silence around them. The giant engine had stopped unexpectedly, failing to drown out the lyrics of the song.

"I told you he'd be trouble," the old lady said from her stool, looking more pleased than scandalized.

Mr. Briscoe fired her a glare forbidding enough to singe thread. She turned back to her loom.

"That's what you find when you get too near the water-front." Mr. Briscoe turned to the gentlemen, pulling Lucky by the collar so that he, too, faced them. "Wharf rats."

Lucky shook off the overseer's hand and straightened, pulling the cotton from his ears. The men examined him as though he were a strange species of fish, newly netted. He felt breathless with fury.

"You see, gentlemen, we try, out of Christian charity, to give some of the colored dregs of our society an opportunity to advance themselves. Sadly, it's rare that they can be reformed."

Lucky gathered himself to his full height, trying to still the pounding in his ears. He licked his lips.

"What chance have you given me?" Lucky asked. "What chance have you given any of us? The chance to lose an arm to one of these machines? The chance to have so much cotton in our lungs that we can't breathe without wheezing?"

Briscoe took a step toward Lucky, hands clenched into fists at his sides. It was clear he wasn't used to being called out. Briscoe was going to strike him. Lucky jumped out of the way. One of the gentlemen cleared his throat and Briscoe stepped back, unclenching his hands in a deliberate manner. "Fortuna," he cried.

But since the fancy gentlemen were there to keep Briscoe in line, Lucky decided he had more he wanted to get off his chest. "Thanks for the opportunity!" he shouted. "Thanks for the show of Christian charity."

Suddenly, Fortuna was at Lucky's side, grasping his arm.

"Remove him from my sight," Briscoe ordered. "And report to me first thing." He waved them away as though the matter had become tiring. "Gentlemen, if you'll follow me, please."

"Go." Fortuna pushed Lucky past the long line of looms and toward the door.

The old lady's eyes sparkled, and the hint of a smile seemed to creep into the corners of her lips. She wasn't the only one. Several of the women nodded at Lucky as he passed.

This seemed to make Fortuna even angrier. Lucky didn't dare glance behind, didn't dare slow for fear Fortuna might slap him.

Then his humiliation would be complete.

But his guardian didn't raise a hand or say a word as they passed through Spinning Room Two. He remained silent as he took his clothes from the bin and dropped his white overalls into the barrel. With clipped movements, Lucky did the same.

Lucky started when the machine roared back to life. Fortuna's face was expressionless as they walked down the stairs and out of the mill.

"You're probably ready to be rid of me," Lucky said as the heavy door slammed behind them.

"Rid of you?" Fortuna's eyes narrowed to slits. "You've only gotten a taste of how miserable your life can be. You'll be working for me 'til you've reached the age of majority."

"But you heard the man. I'm not welcome at the mill anymore."

Fortuna sneered at him. "You think I'd let that fool Briscoe ruin my plans?" He spit a wad of tobacco into the air. It landed on the cobbles with a splat. "In this life you have to take what you want. No one's going to give it to you."

"What about me? What about what I want?"

Fortuna laughed with genuine pleasure. "Not my worry. You came as a boon to me. I like to think the tide brought you as a gift. Your wages, pittance though they were, made more for me. I'd have been simpleminded not to take advantage of the opportunity."

"Hell's bells, my life is your opportunity? What about me?"

"What about you?"

"Now that I'm finished at the mill, I'd say I'm no longer a boon."

Fortuna smiled, displaying the full front row of his peg teeth. Lucky noticed for the first time how the tobacco had started to stain their edges.

"You're wrong, *menino*. Though you've not done well here, 'tis true." Fortuna grabbed Lucky's ear and yanked. "I'll have no more of your nonsense and disobedience when we get to Lowell."

"Lowell?"

"What did you think, that I'd allow you to slither back into the sea? There's work aplenty in Lowell and at a day's journey from the sea, there's not so much riffraff around either." He nodded toward the docks.

Lucky swallowed hard. If he were in Lowell, how would he secure his bargain with Emmeline and get onto Captain Mayhew's ship? All the plans he'd made would evaporate like water on hot deck planks. He bit his lip and searched the horizon for an answer. But all he saw were gulls circling.

He took a furtive glance at Fortuna, willing his own eyes to stay blank, hopeless. But Fortuna's attention was on the line of workers filing out of the mill.

Lucky watched how his eyes changed when he saw her. Alice broke away from the line and made her way toward them, her face pale.

"Stay here," Fortuna warned as he started toward her. "I'll be watching."

But when the first group of workers got thick around him, Lucky seized the opportunity and bolted.

Heading east toward the waterfront, he kept running past the workshops where coopers pounded barrels, caulkers sealed seams, and sail lofts gave life to expanses of canvas like enormous white wings. Tall masts crowded the harbor where the wharves were lined with barrel upon barrel, cask upon cask, too many to count.

Bells started ringing in the distance and Lucky squinted up to the hill. The sound was out of place and disorienting, as though the peals called out a warning whose meaning was hidden.

Lucky kept running. He didn't stop until he got to the weed-choked throughway of the abandoned wharf. Hopefully, Raab would be sober.

He headed down the wharf toward the shack where Raab liked to sit. He was there, all right. Cap pulled down over his eyes, slumped atop a crate, and basking in the late afternoon sun.

Not wanting to startle him, Lucky crept forward. The brig where he'd taught Daniel to swim leaned even more precariously to her starboard side, as though one puff of wind and she'd collapse.

"Sir," Lucky tried to keep his voice low, but it cracked with urgency. He held his hands behind him to keep from reaching out and shaking the old sailor awake.

Raab's breathing was deep and he snored slightly. His right hand rested where his knee would have been.

"Raab," Lucky tried again, a bit louder, peering back over his shoulder.

The old man sputtered awake. "What? What'd you want?"

"I need your help." Lucky crouched and scanned the waterfront for any sign of Fortuna. Surely, his guardian was already searching for him.

"Oh, 'tis you, lad." He put the hat back over his eyes.

Lucky thought he might have gone back to sleep. "I said I need your help, one sailor to another."

Raab removed the cap again, irritation showing in the way he drew his brows together over red eyes. "If it's help yer wanting, better ask an able-bodied man. Cripple like me can't do much to help anyone."

"But you said you knew where to find things."

"What is it ye seek?"

"I need sailor's protection papers."

"You and a boatload of others," he said, yawning.

"I'll have to go to Lowell if I can't get some. I'll lose my chance to go to sea."

"Those papers come at a hefty price." Suddenly Raab was wide awake. "You got money?"

Lucky shifted, his gaze straying to the listing brig. He had only one possession of value. His palms felt hot at the thought of the knife, hidden in his bunkroom at Mrs. Cabral's. It was the only way. Surely, Pa would have understood. Lucky took a deep breath. "I've got something to trade," he said.

"Let's see it."

"Don't have it with me. It's my pa's knife."

"Get it and come back."

"Then you can get the papers?"

"I can get you anything you want, if the price is met."

Lucky eyed him suspiciously. He thought of what Daniel had said about not being able to trust a man who drank before supper. Lucky had certainly seen his share of sailors back in port less than three days and already separated from their pay for three years' work. Poured down the neck of a bottle. He'd make sure he saw the papers before he handed over the knife to Raab. He had to act fast, or it would be too late. There was no more time for Quaker causes or bargains, and no more time to worry about anyone but himself.

"I'll be back," he said and ran toward Fayal.

People whispered to each other in the streets. Groups gathered on the corners and shopkeepers stood outside their doors and surveyed passersby.

Must have been some tragedy, Lucky thought. Some bigwig died or some such. He glanced up the flagpole at the Customs House as he ran past, but the flag hung limp at the top. He'd just crossed Union Street when he heard someone call his name.

Emmeline waved with one hand, using the other to lift the hem of her long black gown as she hurried down the street toward him.

What in the blue blazes was she doing here? Any moment he stood still was one Fortuna could use to catch him. But since she was already here, he might as well tell her what had happened. He owed her that much, anyway.

Emmeline caught up with him. "Praise be," she said, "I've been looking all over creation for thee."

"How'd you find me?"

"It's of no consequence," she said, taking up his hand. "We haven't much time. They're coming."

"Who's coming?"

She gripped his hand more forcefully and pulled. "The kidnappers!"

Lucky's stomach dropped as though weighed down by an anchor. "How d'you know they're coming?"

"Word came from Boston. We must hurry!"

Lucky realized what course her compass was set on: his promise to lead the escaped slaves to safety. How had he ever been roped into that?

"Where's your uncle?"

"In Boston."

He squinted hard at her. "Do you even have an uncle?"

Emmeline's mouth dropped open. She couldn't have looked more hurt or surprised if Lucky had slapped her.

"I'm sorry," he said. "I didn't mean it." He continued, changing tack. "But I disbelieve that a ship of slave catchers could sail into port and start rounding up fugitives. How would they be able to tell them from the Cape Verdeans and other free colored?"

"That's not how they operate! They sneak in and do their kidnapping by the light of the moon."

He planted his feet firmly on the street. "Things have changed, Emmeline. I can't help you. I've troubles of my own."

"What troubles?"

"I was fired from the mill. Fortuna says we're going to Lowell tomorrow. So I'm sorry that I can't help you, but there's no time. I've got to leave town now."

Her gaze clouded. "There's more at stake than thine own future. They're not going on a pleasure cruise, Lucky. Those who don't die on the voyage back or at the hands of their angry masters are returning to a life of slavery. Is that what thou wouldst want for thy friend from the mill?"

Lucky turned to escape her searching eyes. "Of course not. But there's nothing I can do. If I stay, Fortuna'll make sure I'm on that train to Lowell."

"Where will thou go?"

"To the wharf. I know someone who can help me ship out."

"How?"

Lucky studied the line of cobbles on the street. "I've arranged to get some papers."

He looked up to find her staring at him. Slowly, realization dawned on her face. Her mouth hung open for a moment then snapped shut. "Sailor's protection papers, no doubt. I should have known," she said in a cold, clipped voice.

Lucky took a deep breath and struggled for words. The accusation showed clear in her eyes: she believed he'd never intended to honor their bargain. "I didn't plan this," he said. "I wanted to ship with your uncle as a full member of the crew."

"And what of the protection papers? Did it occur to thee that they might be used to save the life of a fugitive? That thy friend Daniel might need them more than thou?"

"Daniel? On a ship?" Lucky tried to laugh but the sound stuck in the back of his throat.

"Why not leave later?" she offered. "After we've helped the fugitives?"

"I told you, I can't." A sudden thought came to him. "Besides, the Fugitive Slave Law says what they're doing is legal."

It had been the wrong argument to use. He knew it as soon as the words left his lips.

Emmeline glanced down at her hand, which was still gripping Lucky's. She thrust it away from her as though it were diseased. "I concern myself with God's law. I'll stay on the right side of that. And who art thou to talk about law? When hast thou worried about breaking any law other than the silly ones made up by thy sailor compatriots?"

"Are you calling the whaleman's commandments stupid?"

"Yes! If used as license to do thy will at the expense of the lives and liberty of others!"

They glared at each other for a long moment.

"Don't tell me I'm the only one who can help. Find someone else to steer your blasted boat!" Lucky glanced up at the sky, which was fast becoming dark. "I've got to go," he said and started toward Mrs. Cabral's.

"Go ahead," she called after him. "Keep chasing thy precious *Nightbird*. And good riddance!"

He turned to reply. She stood on the corner looking like a captain facing a mutinous crew, with chin in the air and fingers curled tight into knotted fists. The words, only half-formed, died on Lucky's lips.

The cry of a lone gull followed him down the street.

Stopper Knot

The afternoon turned windy as Lucky made his way back to the boardinghouse. Clouds of dust rose like phantoms and swirled down the street. He crept through the back alley that led to Mrs. Cabral's garden and climbed the fence.

The back door was unbolted but the landlady didn't answer when Lucky called. The house was quiet and the spicy smell of chachupa hung in the air. He ran up the stairs and into his room, grabbed at the mattress, and found the knife hidden behind the bedpost, just where he'd left it.

He ran his fingers over the handle, willing the etched lines into his memory. Soon, that memory would be all he'd have left of Pa's knife. That is, if all went as planned. Would the knife be enough to buy the protection papers? He gazed around the room. The few articles of his clothing Fortuna had given back were worthless. There was nothing else of value.

Lucky thought for a moment about asking Mrs. Cabral for help. But he didn't know if he could risk telling her what he planned. No matter, she wasn't around anyway. Was he desperate enough to break whaleman's commandment #1? No, he shook his head to banish the thought. Emmeline might say otherwise, but he did have his morals. Stooping that low would put him in the same boat with Fortuna. No, he'd do many things, but he'd not steal from a friend.

He tucked the knife into the back of his trousers so it rested at the small of his back. The blade felt cool and reassuring against his skin. Just having Pa's knife near made him feel stronger and more resolved. He made sure his shirt concealed the ivory handle and left the room.

On his way downstairs he heard clomping footsteps outside. Someone was approaching the front door. Fortuna? There was a knock, then another, louder and louder. The hall tree with its many coats and hats vibrated with the banging, as if it would come to life and reach up to wrap Lucky in its heavy limbs.

"Lucky!"

He pushed the door open and pulled Daniel inside. "I thought you were Fortuna!"

Daniel lowered his head and took three gasping breaths. "I had to find you. Didn't know what else to do."

"Did you hear about what happened at the mill?"

"Everybody heard. But that's not—"

"Lowell!" Lucky interrupted.

"What?"

"We're to leave for Lowell first thing in the morning!"

"Who?"

"Me and Fortuna!" Lucky leaned closer. Daniel's face didn't look quite right. His skin had taken on a yellow pallor. "You've not paid attention to a word I've said. What's wrong with you?"

"Jessup's here," Daniel said, opening the door a crack and peering out of into the street.

"Jessup?"

Daniel eased the door shut and turned to face him. "My old master's overseer. Come to get me, just like he said he would."

Lucky whistled. "You saw him?"

"No. Smelled his pipe smoke outside the Customs House."

Lucky puzzled over this for a moment. "I bet a hundred fat cat bankers smoke the same tobacco."

Daniel shook his head. "It was Jessup. I know it."

"Those abolitionists have you scared of your own shadow. There aren't any slave catchers here. And even if any come, I'm sure they wouldn't bring an old overseer from all the way down in Alabama!" Lucky laid a hand on Daniel's shoulder. "I'm the one who's got real trouble. If I don't find some way out of here, I'm bound for Lowell. I'll be stuck working for Fortuna for years!"

Daniel stared. "It's Jessup."

"What do ya want me to do? Go get the law onto every pipe-smoking so-and-so who chances out onto the public thoroughfares?"

Daniel's shoulders sagged. He pulled away from Lucky's touch. "Guess I'd better get going." He turned and took a step toward the door.

Lucky drew in his breath, wishing he could take back the

words and swallow them whole, like the whale'd swallowed Jonah. He was sure his friend was mistaken. But if Daniel believed Jessup might be in town, Lucky couldn't leave him to face his fate alone. They were both trying to escape their tormentors. What they needed was a plan.

"Wait." Lucky reached for his friend's arm again but Daniel stepped away.

"No," he said. "You've got your own problems. It's not right, me coming to you with mine."

"The way I see it," insisted Lucky, "we have the same problem. I have an idea."

"What?"

Lucky stepped over to the enormous hall tree with its assortment of hats, caps, and capes. He took a black bonnet and placed it on Daniel's head. "There."

Daniel snatched the hat from his head. "This ain't no time to be foolin' around!"

"I'm not playing," Lucky said. "I have a plan." He pulled a shawl from one of the lower hooks. "Not just the hat. Here, let's get you disguised." He put the lacy shawl around Daniel.

"Not a chance," Daniel said, peering into the wavy glass of the mirror. "I look like a boy with a women's hat and wrap on."

Lucky squinted at his friend and had to admit he was right. A bonnet and shawl were not enough. It would take full ladies' kit.

"I know," Lucky said, and dashed up the stairs.

He ran to his room and threw open the trunk where Mrs.

Cabral stored her old gowns. He pulled out a long black dress which had clearly not fit the landlady for a long, long time. It must have been from the time before she lost her arm, for it had intact long black sleeves. Lucky held it up. Though it was far too small for Mrs. Cabral, it looked about right for Daniel. He rummaged through the trunk and grabbed another black gown. Humming a chantey, he gathered both dresses in his arms and headed down the hallway toward the stairs.

A crash below stopped him in his tracks.

Daniel, still wearing the bonnet and shawl, struggled with a man in the foyer. His back was toward Lucky, but there was no mistaking the tall figure. Antone!

Without stopping to think, Lucky glided down the stairs. When he reached the bottom, he rushed at Antone, throwing the skirt of one of the dresses over his head like a sack.

"Get his arms!" Lucky cried as the black fabric ballooned over Daniel's attacker.

"Hey!" Antone shouted and tried to turn on him, but was hit with a fit of coughing.

Lucky had already launched himself onto Antone's back. They fell to the floor with a thud.

Daniel jumped on the fallen man and together they held the dress over his upper body. "What now?" he yelled as Antone bucked beneath him, alternating between wheezing and cursing.

"We'll have to get him to the cellar," Lucky searched for something to tie his arms. "Don't let go," he warned, grabbing the shawl, which had fallen off Daniel in the struggle, and wrapping it the best he could around Antone.

"Drag him by his feet," Lucky said. But Antone started kicking. Desperately scanning the hallway, Lucky spied the cast-iron tray that collected water from dripping umbrellas. The branches of hats and caps shook as he grabbed the tray and, *Wham.* The tray struck bone.

The hallway was quiet.

"If we can get him to the cellar stairs," Lucky said, wiping sweat from his forehead, "there'll be a metal bolt between him and us in case he comes to before we're gone."

Daniel nodded, his eyes wide.

As they dragged Antone toward the cellar, Lucky couldn't help goading the unconscious man. "How d'you like being shanghaied, you son of a sea cook?"

They laid him face down at the top of the stairs and Lucky pulled the dress from Antone's head. He held it up and was relieved to see it hadn't ripped. "Take his belt off and bind his arms with it," he ordered Daniel.

Daniel took the belt, and Lucky began taking Antone's pants off.

Daniel eyed him quizzically.

"Hell's bells! You may think we look silly dressed as girls, but he'd look even sillier chasing us down the street with no trousers on."

Back in front of the hall tree mirror, Daniel struggled to fit the dress over his clothes while Lucky bolted back upstairs for another shawl.

He'd made it halfway back down before he saw her.

She must have come in quietly through the back door. Daniel stood at the mirror, oblivious to her presence, trying to get the front of his gown laced. A stray beam of afternoon light shone in through the transom over the door, illuminating the bonnet on Daniel's head as if it were a halo.

Lucky started to speak, but something about the way Mrs. Cabral gazed at Daniel stopped him. He stood frozen on the stairs, riveted to the expression on her face.

Daniel was quite a sight, Lucky thought. The bonnet and shawl concealed his face. And other than the fact that it would not button over Daniel's shirt, the gown fit perfectly. Its hem fell just right to hide the leather boots.

Mrs. Cabral's features displayed a strange mix of fear, surprise, and something else. It was as though she'd seen…a ghost.

"Beulah?" she said, so quietly that Daniel didn't hear. But her voice reached Lucky, and held him where he stood. It sounded so young and full of hope. It was as though she were a different person.

She stepped forward slowly, as if in some kind of trance.

Daniel turned to face her.

And the spell was broken.

In that moment, before she noticed him, Lucky saw her catch her breath.

Then she stood tall and was all business.

"What's going on here?" she asked, sounding surprised but not angry.

Lucky bounded down the stairs. All of the excuses he should have had on the tip of his tongue eluded him. "Nothing," was all he could manage. Then an idea occurred to him and he added, "Daniel was feeling poorly and I thought he might borrow some warm clothes."

She raised her eyebrows and grabbed the end of her stump with her good hand. It was her version of crossing her arms. "I lost my arm, not my mind," she said, taking the shawl from Lucky and setting it on a table to the right of the door. "You think I didn't hear the bells ringing and see the commotion down by the waterfront? Heard all about the bounty hunters headed this way. I can see why you'd like to avoid running into them. 'Specially you." She nodded toward Daniel.

"Daniel saw a man who works for his old master." Lucky blurted out the half-truth.

"I saw your half brother," Mrs. Cabral said.

"Where?"

"Down by the waterfront. In quite a state. Asked me if I'd seen you."

"What'd you tell him?"

"Told him 'twas clear as day you had the sea in your blood, just as sure as your pa. Said I'd not be surprised if you'd stowed away on the first ship heading out."

Lucky breathed easier, but only for a moment. "He'll still be looking down at the waterfront."

"Is that where you're planning to go?" Daniel asked.

Lucky nodded. "If we can get out of here, you should head straight to Pleasant Street and join the others."

"What others?"

"The fugitives."

But before Lucky could explain, a pounding commenced in the hallway. It was the cellar door.

129

Lucky and Daniel gaped at each other.

"What in creation?" Mrs. Cabral said.

"I can explicate," Lucky said. "We ran into some trouble and had to fend off a no-account mulespinner by the name of Antone. He's Fortuna's henchman."

"You decided it would be a good idea to lock him in my cellar?" Mrs. Cabral didn't sound angry, at least not exactly.

"He grabbed Daniel, and would've taken me, too, if we hadn't stopped him." Lucky shrugged. "I'm sorry, Mrs. Cabral. I didn't mean to break up your place. Maybe it's best if we go now."

"Hmmm. I've got an idea. What do you think, Beulah?" She nodded, then smiled and strode toward the hall. "We'll do what we can, won't we, Beulah?" Her words drifted after her followed by more mutterings, which Lucky decided must be meant just for Beulah.

"Is she all there?" Daniel asked when she was gone, tapping a finger to his temple.

Lucky was relieved to see Daniel looking like himself again. "Yeah," he said. "She is."

Mrs. Cabral's voice carried from the hallway. "You pipe down, or I'll have the law on you, hear?"

"Let me out!" came Antone's muffled reply.

"I run a respectable establishment," she continued as though she hadn't heard him. " I can't have ruffians barging in and interfering with my guests."

"I'm the one interfered with!" Antone's shout was interrupted by a coughing fit. "That errand boy of yours knocked me over the head!"

130

"Be that as it may," Mrs. Cabral's voice was soothing, "You'll have to wait while I find the key. Now don't break anything, or the constable will be here directly."

"Hell's bells," Lucky said as she glided back down the hall toward them.

"I'll let him out after you boys have gotten a good start," she said.

"You may want to give him these." Lucky handed her Antone's trousers.

"Thank you, ma'am, for helping us and for the use of your clothes," Daniel said.

"You're welcome, I'm sure. But these aren't mine. No, siree. You'd swim in my clothes," she said. "These dresses are Beulah's."

Lucky stared at her in astonished silence. "But...but I thought..."

"You thought what?" she asked as she tightened the stays on the bodice of his gown.

Lucky hesitated for a moment, but there was no delicate way to put it. "I thought Beulah was the name you'd given your missing hand."

She gazed at her stump for a moment. "I miss Beulah far more than that hand." Then she shook her head and gave a sad smile. "Beulah's my daughter, gone these fifteen years."

For a moment Lucky couldn't think, couldn't speak.

"You must miss her something powerful," Daniel said after an awkward silence. "Is that why you talk to her?"

Mrs. Cabral shrugged. "I suppose. Folks may think I'm a

crazy old woman, but she's here." She put her hand on her heart. "Sure as my right hand ain't."

Lucky's gown was nearly laced. He took a deep breath and held his hands out in front of him. Blast it! Their ruse would never work, he realized, staring down at his callused and oily fingers.

Mrs. Cabral tutted at the sight. "You get your friend's dress laced. I have something for those mill worker hands."

She headed up the stairs.

"Take your shirt off," Lucky ordered.

"I'll keep my shirt, thank you." Daniel took a step back.

"There's not room for it under the dress," Lucky said. "Off with it."

Daniel retreated another step, his back almost touching the wall. "All right." His voice cracked strangely as he spoke. He yanked his shirt off and threw Beulah's dress over his head. "You happy now?"

"No." Lucky stepped forward. They didn't have time for games. Why was Daniel acting so strangely? "Yours comes together aft; I'll have to help." He turned Daniel by the shoulders and grabbed for the laces of the bodice.

"Don't," Daniel shouted, his voice unnaturally high. But it was too late.

Throat Seizing

L ucky's hands froze. Layered like a crude lattice pattern across Daniel's back were a collection of angry red welts. Under these were older scars, white snaking lines, raised like cords of rope. Lucky'd seen men get lashed before. But never anything like this.

Daniel lurched forward, yanking the fabric out of Lucky's hands. Then he stood very still, head down and breathing heavily.

"Who did this?' Lucky asked in a hoarse whisper.

"Jessup," Daniel said. He reached behind him and pulled the fabric of the dress together.

"For what?"

"One thing or another," Daniel snapped. "Didn't always say."

Lucky lowered his hands and took a deep breath. He forced his fingers back into motion, as if by lacing the stays on Daniel's gown he could somehow loosen the knot which had tightened around his gut. His hands trembled as he completed the task. Lucky struggled to find the right words to say, but none would come. All he could think of were the floggings he'd seen at sea: hardened sailors reduced to tears by a few bites of the lash. All thoughts of Fortuna, Lowell, and the mill faded. Lucky closed his eyes, but the image of the whipping scars lingered, a terrible map of what the future might hold.

As the uncomfortable silence stretched on, small black lengths of fabric fluttered down into the landing like a flock of ravens. One landed on Lucky. He glanced down and shuddered at the sight of thin black fingers on his shoulder, as though poised to grab hold.

"Gloves!" Daniel cried, a smile warming his face.

Lucky relaxed a bit, but the knot in his belly failed to ease. He followed Daniel's lead and put the gloves on. Now, at least, their hands wouldn't give them away.

When Daniel was finished dressing, he put his hands on his hips. Lucky stared at him in disbelief. "You make a real sissy-looking girl," he said.

Daniel gave him a half smile. "You sure are an ugly old lady."

"I expect you'll both do," Mrs. Cabral said, huffing a bit as she descended the staircase.

A shutter banged against the house and Lucky bit his lip. The afternoon would soon turn to evening. "Come on," he told Daniel. "We need to get moving."

"Where to?"

But Lucky was still working on a plan. He shrugged. Best he not say too much in front of Mrs. Cabral, anyway. That way she wouldn't have to lie if Fortuna showed up.

On his way out the door, she handed Daniel a black silk parasol.

"Mrs. Cabral…," Lucky started, but his throat threatened to close over his voice.

She hugged him to her, and he took a deep breath that smelled of earth and soap. "You can thank me by making good use of your talents. Don't waste what you've learned." She opened the door a crack, checked the street, and motioned to them.

Lucky held onto the banister as he made his way down the stairs, careful not to trip over the hem of the gown. He worked Mrs. Cabral's words like a rigger worked a tough knot. What could she have meant? He glanced back, hoping to get a clue from her expression. But the door was already shut.

The sidewalks were unusually crowded for this time of day. But the wind was full of sand, which churned through the air, causing folks to squint and cover their eyes. No one seemed to pay much attention to a pair of ladies making their way down South Water Street.

A gull cried. Lucky pushed the shawl higher and looked up to see Delph circling overhead.

"Wish I could figure that bird out," he said to Daniel. "Knows us even dressed like this."

The corners of Daniel's mouth turned up but the smile didn't reach his eyes. Tension showed in the little line that formed between his brows. "That's one for the Hereafter," he said absently as he scanned the pressing crowds and opened the parasol.

"We're better off like this, packed like fish in a barrel," Lucky said. "Fortuna's less likely to spot us."

"Mayhap," Daniel whispered in too-high a voice. Was he

trying to sound like a girl? Lucky peered at him, but the black silk obscured his face.

A large crowd gathered to the east, at the corner of Walnut and Front Streets. Lucky turned that way but Daniel resisted, pulling him north instead.

"Someone over there can tell us what's going on."

"All right," Daniel relented, "but pull your shawl down and bend your back. You're walking more like a sailor than a decrepit old woman."

His friend's nerves were pulled tight as a triple-loop knot. If Daniel couldn't relax, he might do something that would give them away. Lucky had an idea. "Guess I'm not good at playing the part. You seem suited to it, though. You've a spring in your step sure to charm any half-sober sailor."

Daniel scowled.

"I'd keep a keen lookout, were I you."

"For what?" Daniel checked behind them as he spoke.

"Lads with number 8 on their minds."

"What's number 8?" he asked.

"Whaleman's commandment #8: 'love as many women as you can catch.' One of those boys might mistake you for a fancy catch."

Daniel stopped and stared at Lucky in disgust.

Now *that* was the Daniel he knew. "Someone's making a speech." Lucky pointed toward the waterfront.

A group gathered at the entrance to one of the wharves, where a man stood on a large barrel and addressed the crowd. He held his hat to his head to keep it from blowing away.

"Within the hour," they heard the man say.

"Where?" someone in the crowd shouted.

"We know not, my good man. There are boats keeping watch in the harbor even now."

"What can we do?" a woman called.

"You'd best keep a vigilant eye, madam. It's possible they're already here, walking among us."

Lucky tapped the shoulder of a boy standing in front of them. He pulled the shawl close so the boy couldn't see his face. "What's all the ruckus?" he asked in his best imitation of a squeaky old crone.

"Kidnappers! Come to capture fugitive slaves and take 'em back south," the boy said excitedly.

Daniel's arm supporting Lucky shook slightly.

The boy leaned close.

"Show some respect," Lucky squeaked.

The youth shifted on his feet. "No disrespect intended, ma'am, but you and your daughter might want to stay indoors. On account of your being colored, I mean. There's to be bad men about, and you ladies don't want to get mixed up in it."

"That's mighty good advice," Lucky squealed. "I've always told my Frances to stay well away from the docks, haven't I, Frances?" When Daniel said nothing, Lucky continued, "Men there have no good on their minds and little money besides." He knew they should be moving on, but being a part of the crowd made Lucky feel safer.

Daniel pinched his arm.

"D'you hear the boy, Frances? We should get well away."

"Yes, Mother," Daniel mumbled as Lucky led him east along the waterfront. "Where are we going?" he whispered.

"We have to blend in with the crowd and get over to Raab's wharf."

"Two ladies all dressed in black on an abandoned wharf? Don't you think that will make folks a mite suspicious?"

Lucky thought for a moment. "You're right. When we get near, you should hide behind one of the pilings. Arouse less notice that way."

Daniel shook his head but allowed Lucky to lead him across the waterfront. The wind was so strong now that the skirts of their gowns billowed like sails.

"Wait here," Lucky pointed to a stout piling at the outer edge of the wharf. He moved as quickly as Beulah's skirt would allow, toward the wall of Raab's shack.

Timber Hitch

But Raab was nowhere to be seen.

Waves splashed against the beams of the ruined ships as if bent on raising their bones from the harbor floor and setting them to sea again.

Lucky paced around the outside of the shack. He needed time to think. He wanted to banish the pictures that clouded his thoughts: the broadside about kidnappers in Boston, the look on Emmeline's face when he told her he was leaving, and finally, the terrible scars on Daniel's back. He closed his eyes tight, but it was as though those scars were burned into the back of his eyelids.

He must plan! Lucky untangled his foot from the hem of the heavy skirt. He'd do the best he could for Daniel, but he needed to get the papers first. He called Raab's name. Once, twice, three times. But only the wind replied, whistling through the loose boards of the structure and causing one of the few remaining shingles to tap against the tar-covered wood beneath.

Lucky circled the windowless building once more and knocked on the sagging door. Nothing. But when he tried the rusted latch, he found it was bolted on the inside. He let out his breath with a sigh of relief. The old sailor must be holed up inside.

"Ahoy." He knocked so hard he thought the decrepit planks might rattle right off their hinges. Raab had to answer. He had to have gotten the papers.

Finally, over the moans of the wind, Lucky thought he heard movement inside.

Metal scraped against metal, and the door opened inward. Raab appeared, his peg attached loosely over his trouser leg.

Lucky stepped forward into the darkness that smelled of damp, mildew, and rum.

In the corner, a lantern cast a flickering yellow glow that exposed a makeshift bunk and several barrels and crates. On one of the barrels, an empty bottle lay on its side.

Raab's eyes were red and bleary. "Missus," he said and bowed his head. Pink scalp showed around the tufts of white hair, making him seem somehow vulnerable. "You've taken a wrong turn and wandered into an unsavory place."

"It's me," Lucky hissed, tearing the shawl from his head. "You got the papers?"

Raab stared at him in disbelief. Had he been drinking? Hard to reckon.

"Do you have my papers?"

"Why're you dressed as a girl?" He scratched at his ear and ran his hand over his face. He looked as though he'd just come out of a deep sleep and couldn't tell whether he was awake yet, or still dreaming.

"Had to get away from my no-account guardian."

"Well, it's a sin to Moses, if you ask me."

"What? Fortuna making me work at the mill?"

"Naw! A sailor dressing as a lady!"

Lucky glanced down at the black gloves. It hadn't occurred to him to be ashamed.

"Might as well kit yourself out in landlubber gear," Raab snorted. A drop of saliva landed on his chin.

Lucky gritted his teeth. "Do you have the papers?"

"Hmmm?"

"The sailor's protection papers." His voice squeaked on the last syllable.

"Ha! You even sound like a girl."

"Do you have them?" Lucky spit the words out one at a time.

"Depends," Raab said. "D'you have the money?"

Lucky's voice rose. "We agreed on a trade."

"We did? I'd prefer cash."

"I don't have any. You knew that. We had an agreement!" Lucky raised his palms, then seeing the gloves, dropped them again to his sides.

"Are you a' saying old Raab isn't a man of his word?"

Lucky lowered his head. His skin prickled under the unfamiliar weight of Beulah's dress. "'Course not, I'm just reminding you, is all."

"I remember," Raab said, wiping at his face with his sleeve. "Now where have those blasted papers gone off to?"

141

He rifled through the contents of a crate to one side of the bunk.

Lucky shifted on his feet and pulled at the neckline of the dress.

"Aha! Knew I'd find 'em. Here!" Raab held up a folded parcel of heavy yellowed paper.

"May I look?"

"Where's the knife?"

"Got it here." Lucky patted the small of his back.

Raab handed him the papers.

"Lucky?" Daniel appeared at the door. He took a step into the room and stumbled forward. Lucky caught him by the arm.

Through narrowed eyes, Raab peered under the bonnet at Daniel. "What in the name of St. Christopher is *he* doing here?"

"He needs to get out, too," Lucky said.

"Unless you've got two of them knives, you're out of luck."

"Maybe we can both use the papers?" Lucky asked.

"Not a chance," Raab shook his head. "You can't go passing 'em about willy-nilly."

"We have to do something. Daniel can't stay in New Bedford either."

"If I was you, sailor, I'd worry about meself. You don't have time or money to be worrying about the fate of land-lubbers."

The old man's words felt like a cold wave striking Lucky's face. He gulped. Hadn't Raab just put a voice to Lucky's very thoughts? Was this the course he'd set his sails for? Was this what he would become? Someone out only for himself? Like Raab?... Like Fortuna? His mouth tasted bitter and his nostrils burned from the smoke and fetid smell of the shack. No, he was not like them!

"Raab's right," Daniel interrupted his thoughts. "Don't worry about me. I'll get on fine."

"No!" Lucky thrust the papers toward Daniel. He heard Emmeline's voice begging for his help. "You take 'em." Emmeline was right.

"Oy." Raab reached for the folded papers. "Plank up, you've not paid."

Daniel backed away. "Paid for what? What is it?"

Lucky hiked his skirt and retrieved the knife. He passed it, handle first, to Raab, lowering the gown as he did so.

"Look here," Lucky said to Daniel, carefully opening the folded pages. "Your name is Larabee Vandiver. You're five foot four inches." He sized up his friend. "Better stand on tiptoes to get 'em to swallow that bait."

"What are you going on about?"

"The sailor's papers." He shook the packet toward Daniel. "These are your ticket on a boat out of here."

"Those are *yours*."

"Not anymore. I want you to have 'em."

"I don't want them."

"Take 'em." Lucky held them out.

"No!" Daniel's voice was firm. He pushed Lucky's hand away. "I'm no sailor. Besides, where would that leave you?"

Raab had watched in stunned silence. "Are you making

the trade or not? There's plenty of others what want these papers if neither of you *ladies* aims to use 'em."

"Thank you, but no." Lucky shook his head. He took Pa's knife from Raab's outstretched hand and thrust the papers forward. Like morning mist lifting from still water, his thoughts were clearing. The scenes in his head were finally sorting themselves into a shipshape order. He'd just been too selfish and afraid to see it before. Lucky backed toward the door.

"What are you going to do now?" Daniel asked, sounding miserable.

"What I should have done in the first place," Lucky said. "I have a bargain to keep."

"Well, I've got better things to do than listen to you ladies argue," Raab said, pushing past them to the door of the shack and opening it wide. The wind tousled the wisps of hair at the sides of his head, making him appear even more disheveled. "In fact, I have an appointment with another lady. Lady Luck's her name. So shove off." He motioned them out.

Lucky lifted his gown and put the knife back.

As he and Daniel left, Lucky tipped Beulah's hat to Raab.

The door slapped shut, and they were alone on the wharf.

"Does this change of heart have something to do with one of your whaleman's commandments?" Daniel asked.

Lucky thought for a moment. "Maybe."

"Which one?" Daniel eyed him warily.

"Number 3." Lucky said, with as much conviction as he

could summon. He tried to smile but there was flotsam doing a jig in his belly. "Fight anytime you think you can w—" His voice cracked. He cleared his throat and tried again. "Win." But the word sounded more like a question.

He pulled Daniel forward.

"Why are we heading away from the waterfront?" Daniel asked as they skirted Union Street in favor of the back alley leading up the hill.

Close Band

T he sky had darkened over the shifting cover of clouds, and though the wind blew stiff out of the northeast, its bite lessened as they moved among New Bedford's buildings.

"We've got to get to Emmeline's before candle-lighting."

"Why?" Daniel asked.

"I made a deal with her. Said I'd get some folks across the river."

"What folks? I thought you were leaving to get away from Fortuna."

Lucky quickened his pace, eager to escape Daniel's eyes. "Changed my mind. Decided not to let Fortuna keep me awash and helpless. I promised Emmeline I'd help the fugitives."

"Like me?" As though reminded of the danger, Daniel scanned the alley on all sides and behind them.

Lucky glanced back. Shirts and trousers hung on lines at the backs of houses. Their arms and legs jerked in the breeze like fish on a hook.

"I'm still not so sure Jessup himself is here." Lucky

shrugged. "But some bounty hunters are, and if they're anything like that bilge rat, we need to get you out of here in a—"

A low growl interrupted what he'd been saying. Something was just out of sight around the corner.

Suddenly, a large gray mutt emerged, whiskers quivering. Seeing Lucky and Daniel, he bounded up and pressed his wet nose against Daniel's skirt.

Lucky bent and held his hand out to the dog. Daniel stood stock still.

"It's only a dog," Lucky chided, as the dog sniffed at him. He petted the creature a few times, then withdrew his hand and sniffed it. "Smells like he's been rolling in three-day-old fish carcasses, but he's not going to hurt ya."

Daniel didn't answer. He stood as if paralyzed.

"If you keep standing there like that, he may mistake you for a tree and lift his leg on your dress."

Daniel's eyes narrowed but he still didn't move. "I'm afraid of dogs," he finally said through his teeth.

"See his tail wagging? What's to be afraid of?"

"Can't help it. Packs of dogs chased me through the swamp. I still hear them barking in my nightmares."

Lucky felt like a no-account fool.

"Here, pup," he said, and picked up a stick. He opened the back fence closest to them and threw it into the yard. When the dog bounded after it, Lucky shut and latched the fence.

They walked the rest of the way to Emmeline's house in silence.

"Stay back," Lucky warned when they emerged from the alley across the street. "There's a carriage at the front."

Hiding in a lilac bush, Lucky and Daniel watched as two ladies in fancy gowns hurried out the massive front door and into the waiting carriage. Bonnets obscured their faces, but there was no mistaking the forceful stride of one of the two. "There goes Emmeline's stepmother," Lucky said, "sure as Christmas."

When the horses had pulled away and were well out of sight, Lucky and Daniel emerged from the bush.

"Should we go around to the back?" Daniel asked in a low voice.

"Nah. Probably got a cook back there, or some other busybody. Best take our chances at the front. Besides, two proper ladies such as ourselves can't be seen crawling around in the shrubbery. It's not proper."

"Your bonnet's on crooked," Daniel said.

Lucky straightened it. "There's mud on your parasol."

Daniel lifted his skirt and wiped the parasol on his trousers.

A woman with a basket of laundry emerged from a side yard and eyed them suspiciously.

Lucky pulled the shawl tighter around his face. "Just having a bit of a gam, dearie," he said in his old lady voice. He took Daniel's arm and steered him down the sidewalk. "Best we get off the street."

When they approached the front steps, Daniel hung back. "Come on," Lucky said, and bounded up to the door. He paused, his hand on a brass knocker in the shape of an anchor. "Here goes," he said with more confidence than he felt, and rapped three times.

In an instant, the door flew open. "Uncle!" Emmeline exclaimed, but her wide grin dropped and transformed to a look of alarm at the sight of Lucky and Daniel.

"May we come in?" Lucky asked.

She didn't answer, but backed away from the door allowing them to enter. Lucky pushed Daniel ahead of him into a wide hallway with Turkish carpets and a curving staircase.

"Lucky?" she finally said.

"In the flesh," he answered closing the door behind them.

Daniel shifted uncomfortably, twirling the dirty parasol.

"Put that down," Lucky ordered. "Don't you know it's bad luck to bring an open umbrella indoors?" Daniel closed the parasol and leaned it against the hall tree.

"What art thou doing here?"

She must have gone all addle-brained at the sight of them in women's dresses, Lucky reasoned, and smiled reassuringly. "Come to keep my part of the bargain," he said.

"What do you mean?" Emmeline asked, still looking bewildered.

"You know. Lead those fugitives down to the river. Heck, I'll row 'em all the way to Fairhaven, if you'd like. Just so long as Daniel can come along."

"Too late," she said, her chin lifting ever so slightly, but enough to let Lucky know she'd remembered the words they'd exchanged earlier. "I'm sorry, Daniel," she added quickly.

"What?" It was Lucky's turn to look bewildered.

"Thou has come too late. They've left already."

"But you said not until well after candle-lighting."

"Plans change, Lucky. Isn't that what you told me?"

He shifted, uncomfortable in the dress. "I'm sorry for what I said earlier. Sorry I wasn't here to help you. I can at least take Daniel to them so he'll be safe from the bounty hunters."

Lucky glanced at Daniel. His friend kept his gaze fixed on the intricate pattern of the Turkish carpet, as though it held a code he must decipher.

She shook her head sadly. "I don't know where they are. One of the other members of the Abolitionist Society led them. He didn't tell me where the ship was docked or where they'd meet it. Said the less we members knew, the easier it would be to answer the law if there were questions later."

"Hell's bells!" Lucky said. "What about your uncle?"

"I don't know what's keeping him," she said miserably. "I thought he'd be here already."

"Can you try to find out where the ship's docked?" Lucky asked. He bit down on his lower lip. If he could just get Daniel to safety with the others. "And do you know where it's headed?"

"Canada, I think."

Well, it wasn't ideal, but Canada would do for him. That is, if they could get to the ship. Lucky took a deep breath.

The rattle of an arriving carriage interrupted his thoughts. Emmeline jumped.

"Maybe it's your uncle," Lucky offered.

"Not in my stepmother's carriage. Hurry, come with me."

Lucky and Daniel followed her down the hall toward the back of the house. Emmeline opened a door and pointed down a dark stairway. "Quickly," she called, leaving them at the top of the stairs, "and close the door behind you."

But it was too dark without the crack of light the open door let in. Lucky left it slightly ajar, to make sure they could see to find their way out again. He thought of Antone and wondered what had happened when Mrs. Cabral let him out. "Hold onto the rail," he whispered to Daniel.

"Don't worry about me." Daniel's voice sounded pinched and afraid.

"We need to get to the bottom." Lucky held the rail with one hand and placed the other along the wall to steady himself. "We can hide—" Suddenly there was a creak of hinges and Lucky felt a rush of air. "What's this?" He seemed to have opened a door in the wall of the staircase.

Tracing the wall with his hand, he found an opening in the planks. A cupboard-type door swung inward to expose a dark space that smelled slightly smoky and of whale oil.

They heard the front door open. Lucky froze.

"Emmeline!" A shrill voice called.

"M-m-mother, I thought thee'd gone to the Ladies Guild meeting."

"I forgot my jeweled reticule. You know how the ladies rely on me to set a standard for the Guild. I couldn't disappoint them."

"Yes, Mother."

There came a disgusted sigh. "Who's come to call?"

"No one, Mother. Thou said I'm not to accept callers."

"Then what is this filthy parasol doing in my vestibule?"

Lucky heard Daniel's sharp intake of breath.

"I plan to offer it to someone in need," Emmeline said.

"I shudder to think what *lady* would find herself in such need that she'd stoop to carry *that* ragged thing," came the reply. The voice became louder as the tap of heels moved down the hallway toward the basement door.

"No, Mother. I'll get thy bag."

"You know I don't want you in my room. What have you been doing in the basement?"

"Nothing, Mother." Emmeline must have reached the door first and shut it firmly.

"Don't push me out of the way!" her stepmother cried.

"I'm sorry, Mother, it's just that I know the ladies are waiting for thee."

"Quick," Lucky took Daniel's arm. "I'll lift you in."

"Don't want to," Daniel murmured.

"We'll be safe," Lucky whispered. "Safer than if Emmeline's stepmother finds us, leastways. If she does, she'll call the law."

Lucky lifted Daniel's skirted legs and pushed him through the opening. Then he jumped in after and pulled the panel closed.

It hadn't been a moment too soon.

"What were you doing down there?" Mrs. Rowland's voice came through the panel. It sounded as if she were at the top of the stairs peering down.

"I heard a noise at the door and thought a cat or some other poor creature might need my help."

"I'll never understand you! It could just as easily have been a rat."

"Yes, Mother." Emmeline said as the door closed. Lucky heard the bolt latch.

They were locked in the basement. Just like Antone had been. Lucky let out the breath he'd been holding.

"I'm sorry about the parasol," Daniel whispered.

Time seemed to stand still in the secret room under the stairs where darkness hung, absolute and smothering. They carried on a whispered conversation for awhile, but Lucky wanted to be able to hear what was going on upstairs. He pushed the door open and stuck his head out. Had Emmeline forgotten them? Had he and Daniel dozed off? Suddenly a lantern shone in his eyes.

"Miss Emmeline?" Daniel said, his voice shaking slightly.

"It's me," she answered. "I'm thankful thou found the secret room!"

"What is this place?" Lucky asked, peering around the illuminated space.

"It's a hidey hole for the Underground Railroad," Emmeline said. "My father had it built years ago. 'Tis a blessing thou found it, or my stepmother might have seen you."

Mention of the Underground Railroad cleared Lucky's thoughts. "What time is it?"

"Nearly ten. I'm sorry! My stepmother was suspicious and insisted I go with her to the meeting. Then she made me stay after for supper."

"Never mind that," Lucky said. "Did you find out about the ship?"

"It's moored off Gull Island."

Daniel let out a low whistle and wiped his hand across his forehead.

Lucky jumped to his feet, banging his head on the ceiling of the tiny room. "I'll find a skiff and row us across."

"Where's your stepmother?" Daniel asked, peering toward the staircase.

"Gone to bed with a headache she claimed I'd given her."

"Is she a sound sleeper?" Lucky whispered.

"She is when she takes Dr. Freeman's Miracle Elixir." Emmeline wrinkled her nose. "I smelled it on her breath. Horrible! I heard my uncle tell Father it's nothing but low-quality corn whiskey sold in a fancy bottle."

Daniel climbed out first and Lucky followed, trying not to hit his head again.

Emmeline led them up the stairs and into the back of the house.

"What time does she sail?" Lucky asked.

"By midnight."

"We'd have a better chance if we shed this women's gear," Lucky said. "Do you think we could borrow a couple of your father's shirts?"

"All Father's clothes are in the room with my step-mother." She held her hand out to Lucky. "Take this," she said, and dropped a small object into his palm.

Lucky's fingers closed around warm metal. He held his hand up to the lantern to look. The knotted brooch that

Emmeline always wore gleamed up at him. He caught his breath and stared at the intricately bound strands of gold as though they were a rigger's knot, a puzzle he could work out. The skin of his palm tingled.

"I can't take this," he said, trying to pass it back to her. "It was your mother's, wasn't it?"

"You may need money," Emmeline said. "'Tis all I have to give. Besides, she'd have given it gladly herself for so worthy a cause."

"We'll take it, then, just in case," Lucky said, blinking hard. "And with thanks. But someday I'll return it to you. I promise." He opened the bodice of his dress and pinned the brooch to the inside, where it wouldn't be seen.

Emmeline opened a door that led into the back garden. She held up the lantern to reveal a series of flower beds surrounded by a circular stone path. "Cut down Walnut Street," she said, "and, Lucky?"

"Yes?" He'd already stepped past her through the door, eager to be on his way. Daniel, close on his heels, bumped into him when he turned.

"Godspeed."

Half-Hitch and Seizing

The sky was a school of fast-moving low clouds. Their long skirts swished and brushed against the cobbles. Lucky felt as though he'd just come ashore in some foreign port and didn't yet have his bearings. He lifted the skirt of Beulah's dress and tried to hurry, with Daniel right behind him.

They stayed close to the shop windows and walked as quickly as possible. Lucky was grateful for his own leather boots under the long skirt. They made no noise and would come in handy if he and Daniel needed to run.

"Are you ladies all right?" A lamplighter carrying a long wooden pole approached, headed toward a burned-out street lamp. "I don't know if you've heard what's been going on, but you really shouldn't be out tonight."

Lucky stepped back into the doorway of a building. He felt Daniel tense beside him and grabbed a handful of fabric at the bustle of his friend's dress. As both a sailor and a Valera, Lucky had a natural affinity for the telling of tales. Daniel did not. Lucky knew his friend would just as soon make a run for it. But pulling foot could endanger them further. They must take their leave gracefully, so as not to arouse the man's suspicions.

He cleared his throat. "We were just taking a stroll after the meeting of the Ladies Sewing Circle," Lucky croaked. "I do find that it does a body good to get some fresh air. Don't you?"

"Not tonight, ma'am. There are some bad men about. Men you wouldn't want to come across."

"Ohhhh." Lucky drew in his breath in an exaggerated gasp. "Do tell!"

"They're kidnappers and slave catchers, ma'am. I assure you, they're men you'd not want to meet in a dark alley…or anywhere else for that matter!"

"We didn't know, did we, daughter?"

Daniel mumbled in agreement.

"Have you come across them?" Lucky asked. "My daughter and I certainly want to avoid running into any unsavory characters."

"Heard they're lurking around the wharves."

"I thank you, my good man. We will return to our lodgings without delay."

Daniel murmured his assent.

"I'd be proud to escort you," the lamplighter said, "just as soon as I get this lantern glowing again."

"Heavens no!" Lucky gushed. "We wouldn't dream of keeping you from your duty of keeping the city of light, er, lit. We'll be plenty safe!"

"Plenty!" Daniel said, and Lucky elbowed him before he could say anything more and end the charade. Already, the man was peering into the darkness, trying to get a better look at them. If they were there when the lamp was re-lit, Lucky didn't like their chances. His heart beat against the tight bodice as he desperately searched his brain for something, anything, to keep the man away.

"Besides," Lucky practically shouted, "my daughter's husband recently came home from sea with a strange and terrible case of New Guinea rat pox fever."

"I'm sorry to hear of your troubles, ma'am," the lamplighter said.

"Thank you. They say it's highly contagious."

The lamplighter took a step away from them.

"But the doctor says he'll probably lose only three of his fingers."

Another step back. "Good evening to you, ladies." Unlit lamp forgotten, the man practically broke into a run in his haste to get away.

"New Guinea rat pox fever?" Daniel asked when he was gone. "Is there really a disease called that?"

"Yup," Lucky said, allowing himself a tight smile. "But it only affects rats."

The lights on the other side of the bridge glowed dimly through the clouds. They approached warily, keeping to the shadows and away from the streetlamps.

"Don't you think we'd best ditch Beulah's dresses?" Lucky asked Daniel for the third time since they'd escaped the lamplighter's attentions.

"Better not. Fortuna, Jessup, and the others ain't looking for two ladies."

"But two ladies dressed in black on a wharf at night? It's bound to arouse some suspicions, don't you think?"

"Yeah. But you made me take off my shirt when I put this on. Unless you got another, what will I wear?"

Lucky winced at the memory of the scars on Daniel's back. "We'll just wait till we meet up with the others. One of them's sure to have some extra shirts."

Daniel said nothing but pointed at the wharf to their right. "That one's got lots of smaller boats tied up. You think there might be one we could borrow?"

It did seem the most likely, Lucky agreed. And there was no sign of anyone about. In fact, it seemed almost strangely quiet. Perhaps, he figured, it was like that once you moved farther upriver, since the big ships tended to dock closer to the entrance of the harbor. It had been a good idea to come here, Lucky congratulated himself. But it might be best if they crossed the bridge where it connected with Fish Island.

"Let's take the bridge," Lucky said. "We'll have our pick of skiffs closer to Gull Island."

"Going somewhere, ladies?" A figure stepped out from behind a stack of barrels not ten feet away.

From the glow of the streetlight behind, his body cut a silhouette which reminded Lucky of a fiddler crab, with one arm longer and bigger than the other.

It was only when he stepped closer that Lucky could make out the long, wide blade of the butcher knife Fortuna held in his right hand.

Cuckolds' Necks

How'd you find us?" Lucky asked. They'd been so careful. Hadn't they cut back and around and checked behind them every move they'd made?

"You wanna find a wharf rat?" Fortuna said. "You go to the wharves."

Lucky glanced over at his friend. Daniel's eyes widened but he said nothing.

"I'll go with you," Lucky said, taking a step toward Fortuna. "Just leave Daniel out of this."

Fortuna's lip rose in a sneer, exposing his peg teeth. He tilted his head and let loose a stream of tobacco. It disappeared onto the black crinoline of Lucky's gown, leaving a warm, wet spot right over his heart.

"Way I figure, he's worth more to me than you are. That is, unless I can convince one of those bounty hunters you're an escaped slave, too." Fortuna's eyes glinted. "Then I could collect two rewards."

"It wouldn't work," Daniel said softly. "No one'd believe Lucky's ever been a slave."

"Shut up." Fortuna reached over with his free hand and slapped Daniel hard.

He didn't even flinch when the blow struck, just stared blankly ahead as if Fortuna weren't there at all. It was as though his mind had gone to a different place. Lucky shivered, more frightened than if Daniel had cried out in pain, though he wasn't sure why. Then he saw the smirk on Fortuna's face and his fear hardened into anger.

"Come on," Fortuna pointed the blade toward the bridge leading across the river to Fairhaven. "Move." He motioned for Lucky and Daniel to walk beside him.

"Where are we going?" Lucky asked, glancing at the harbor. He had an idea. If he could just signal to Daniel, there might still be a way out of this mess. He gazed hard at the bridge, trying to judge the distance to the water below.

"To Fairhaven. Are you that stupid?"

"You can at least put the knife away," Lucky said.

Fortuna held up the blade and examined it. "A sight better than that sorry toy you got from our father, isn't it?"

Thinking about how Fortuna had sold Pa's knife made the knot in Lucky's stomach grow. "What did Pa ever do to you?"

Fortuna let out a humorless bark of laughter. "Wasn't around long enough to do much," he said.

"If you'd known him better, you'd feel differently." The wind had picked up again and Lucky had to raise his voice.

"Wonder what he'd think of you, little brother, all dressed up as a girl? Ha! I wish he could see you now. Do you think he'd be proud? Think he'd call you daughter?"

Lucky bit down on the side of his cheek to keep a wisecrack reply from spilling out. He shot a glance at Daniel, nodding ever so slightly toward the water as they stepped onto the bridge. Fortuna seemed to be awaiting a reply, so Lucky said, "He'd probably have a good laugh at my expense."

"A laugh? That's not the man I knew. He'd have walloped you."

"Maybe," Lucky admitted. *Only if he'd been drinking*, he thought. He peered over at Daniel and, as he trudged forward, swung his right hand toward the side of the bridge and the harbor beyond, pointing as best he could without being too obvious. Did Daniel understand?

A gull flew low overhead, calling a long series of staccato squalls.

Delph? Lucky wondered, as his eyes met Daniel's. He motioned quickly toward the edge of the bridge.

"Fool bird!" Fortuna cried as the gull wheeled and circled. He waved the blade in the air.

"We must have disturbed its nest," Lucky offered. *This is our chance*, he thought.

"What bird builds a nest in the middle of a bridge?" Fortuna leaned down to pick up a pebble. He threw it in the bird's direction but missed.

When he bent again, Lucky was ready. He planted his foot on Fortuna's backside and pushed. Fortuna cried out and stumbled, but didn't completely lose his balance. As he struggled to right himself, his thick boot caught between the planks and tripped him. The knife clattered to the ground.

"Jump, Daniel!" Lucky cried, and hurled himself over the rail.

And then he was falling, slipping into the darkness. The

moment stretched and Lucky's body tensed, bracing for the impact he knew would come.

He met the water with a hard clap. Immediately it enveloped him, and he found himself sinking down into its cool, murky depths. The weight of the dress dragged him like an anchor. To Lucky's surprise, the sensation was not at all unpleasant. How easy it would be to yield to the gentle pressure of the water on his face, his arms and legs, and just allow himself to drift.

But when his feet touched the rocky riverbed, he remembered Daniel. He tried to push off the bottom, but the weight of the wet cloth held him down. Lucky kicked and clawed, but the skirt, which had blown up like a jellyfish and cushioned his descent, now wrapped around him like a shroud. The more he struggled, the more tightly it held. In that instant Lucky realized that *this* was what it felt like to drown. He kicked harder.

Suddenly, his left foot found a hold in fabric. He felt a tug at his waist as the threads of Beulah's gown gave way and tore. Lucky clawed at the torn skirt until he was free.

Three hard strokes and he was at the surface, gasping for breath. He looked around for Daniel, but saw only an unbroken blanket of dark water.

Panic rising, Lucky prepared to dive. He lifted his head to take a deep breath, his eyes straying to the bridge above him.

There, standing at the railing and glaring down at him, was Fortuna. And in front of Fortuna, butcher knife held against his throat, stood Daniel.

Twin waves of relief and dismay washed over Lucky in quick succession. He checked the back of his trousers for Pa's knife and felt the reassuring weight of the small blade still wedged there.

"Climb up!" Fortuna nodded at a ladder that was attached to one of the stone columns supporting the bridge.

Lucky swam over and heaved himself up the first few rungs. The skirt had torn about six inches down from the bodice, leaving a garment midthigh length. *At least Pa's knife is still hidden,* he thought as he climbed up onto the bridge.

"What a shame," Fortuna said as Lucky stood, dripping, in front of him. "You ruined your pretty dress."

Daniel did not look up.

"Now the wharf rat is a drowned rat," Fortuna mocked.

Lucky hung his head. He felt the tip of the butcher knife against his stomach.

"Try something like that again and I'll gut you like a cod." The blade moved slightly and bit through fabric. But instead of hitting flesh, it brushed against Emmeline's brooch. Lucky stood still, willing himself not to shrink back. After a long moment, Fortuna took the blade and pointed east. "Now move," he said.

Lucky's boots squished and bled water with every step. He glanced over at his friend, but Daniel kept his eyes trained on the bridge under his feet. Hell's bells! If Daniel hadn't been too chicken to jump when given the chance, they'd be well away from here and safe.

But no sooner had the thought occurred to Lucky than

the wind turned his emotions in another direction. Guilt. Until just a few weeks ago, Daniel had never swum a stroke in his life. Not only that, but he'd been afraid of the water. And what was another thing Daniel had said he was afraid of? Heights.

Lucky shook his head and a rush of warm water dripped out of his left ear. How could he have been so addle-brained? His plan to escape had been doomed from the beginning.

They had crossed the bridge and stepped onto a wharf on the other side. Fortuna led them along until they were beside an old whaling bark Lucky had never seen before.

Fortuna held out a hand for them to stop and took a step forward, knife drawn. Lucky felt a tide of panic soak through his wet clothes. He shivered, though the night was warm. Whatever Fortuna's plans, if they were thwarted, he just might slit Lucky's throat. And why not here on this dark pier, where none would witness the murder?

"Not a word," Fortuna cautioned. He turned to the hull of the old ship and knocked three times with the blunt han-dle of the knife.

Lucky took a deep breath.

A moment later, a lantern shone over the rail. Lucky glimpsed the outline of two dark figures, but their faces were hidden in shadow. There came a scraping of wood against wood as a gangplank was lowered from the ship.

"I'll not come aboard," Fortuna called, loud and fast.

"I don't do business on public docks," a voice from above replied. "Come aboard or be gone."

Fortuna stood motionless for a moment, seeming to weigh his options. "Go!" he snapped at Lucky and waved the knife at the plank. "Now, you," Fortuna said to Daniel when Lucky had started across.

A rough hand pulled the boys onto the deck. Though the rocking of the ship was at first soothing, Lucky soon sensed something about her wasn't quite right.

The smells were all wrong. The smoky perfume of burnt whale oil, which soaked to the core of a whaleship, was missing. Instead, a sourness rose from these deck boards and hung in the air. Like a mix of vomit and something else Lucky couldn't quite put his finger on.

He turned to Daniel, who stood beside him. He must have smelled it, too, for Daniel's shoulders rose to protect his neck and he crouched as though waiting for someone to strike him.

Fortuna's feet landed on the deck behind them with a dull thud. Immediately, he began to sway and the sweat on his face seemed to glow in the lamplight. Lucky could swear his half brother looked sick.

"What have we here?" A voice rich as velvet drawled from the shadows.

Daniel winced. Fortuna squinted in the direction of the voice and up to the swinging lantern. "Just like I told you at the tavern, I have the boy you're looking for."

"So I see," the man said. He took the lantern from its hook and held it close to them.

Lucky squinted. Beside him, he felt Daniel tremble.

"I got him for you and am here to collect the reward."

Fortuna shielded his eyes from the bright glow of the lantern. With each rock of the ship, Fortuna planted his feet farther apart. What was wrong with him?

"Who's the other girlie boy?" the man with the lantern asked.

"Thought you might want to take him where you're going, too," Fortuna said.

Lucky's eyes had gotten accustomed to the light and he could see the man better now. Short and of slight build, he had yellow hair, which he wore shoulder length, parted in the middle. The hand that trained the lantern on them had small, tapered fingers with well-manicured nails. The other hand held an ebony pipe, carved in the figure of a human head.

It was only then that Lucky realized that part of the smell he'd puzzled over was that of an unusual mix of pipe tobacco.

The man was Jessup!

"The little colored boy's going somewhere, all right," Jessup said with a laugh. "To the sunny South, where the cotton fields stretch as far as the eye can see. He's going home, where he belongs."

"How 'bout the other one?" Fortuna said. "You got any use for him?"

"What can he do? Looks too scrawny to be a good worker."

"He can work in a mill," Fortuna offered. "Your boy's been teaching him."

"How much?" Jessup asked.

"I'd let you have him for five hundred."

Jessup laughed again, a harsh high sound. "Not worth more'n a hundred to me."

"Never mind, then. He's worth more than that to me," Fortuna said.

"You're mighty uppity for a colored boy," Jessup said to Fortuna, his voice amiable.

"I'm Cape Verdean," Fortuna said. "Portuguese." Lucky heard the warning in his voice.

"My apologies." Jessup laughed and beckoned to one of his crew behind them. He drew a pouch from his pocket and added some tobacco to his pipe. "But you're only a shade lighter than that one." He pointed at Lucky with the pipe. Daniel trembled beside him as Jessup puffed a cloud of sickly sweet smoke. "And a shade don't mean much where we're going."

A heavy wooden club came out of the darkness. Before Lucky had time to react, it came down on Fortuna's head.

"'Cept maybe a higher price." Jessup laughed.

Fortuna lay sprawled unconscious on the deck.

Seized Shortening

C aptain," Jessup said, "kindly have your men tie them up and throw them into the hold. Not too roughly, mind. I'll not have them damaging my goods. Especially not after what happened in Boston."

"Yessir, Mr. Jessup." Lucky gazed up in surprise. What manner of master allowed someone to boss him around on his own ship? This captain had no posture of authority. His shabby, rumpled clothes said deckhand, and his voice shook as though from drink. What kind of ship was this?

As Lucky tried to get a better measure of the man, he was spun roughly to his side, wrists pulled behind his back.

"This one here's all wet," the deckhand who held him protested.

"Then let him stay that way," Jessup said.

"I don't want to get wet," the man mumbled grumpily as he bound Lucky's wrists. Lucky let his breath out slowly through his nose. He held his wrists as far as he could from the wet fabric, all the while praying Pa's knife would pass undetected.

"I'm expecting several more *visitors* before we leave port tomorrow, Captain. Then, I'll be ready to head straight to Providence."

"Aye, Mr. Jessup."

Fortuna was carried and Lucky and Daniel were pushed over to the hatch leading down to the ship's hold. The wooden panel was opened, and Fortuna was lowered first. His body thumped onto the deck below.

Lucky and Daniel made it down the ladder as best they could with their hands tied behind them.

A moment later, the hatch was closed, leaving them in complete and utter darkness.

The wind had picked up again, and the ship rolled. Lucky thought he might be sick. The horrible smell from above decks was much worse below.

Lucky could no longer stand the weight of the silence. "I don't know what business that sorry excuse for a captain does, but this ship's not brought in a whale for a long, long time."

Daniel made a sound in the darkness. Lucky thought he might be too stirred up to speak.

"It's not a whaleship, Lucky," he finally said, his voice sounding flat and tired.

An ache of dread had crept into Lucky's bones. "What is it, then?"

"It's a slaver."

Lucky turned sharply to the sound of Daniel's voice. "How'd you know that?"

"The smell," he said quietly. "Mama told me slave ships

reek of sick, fear, and despair. She was on one when she was a little girl. Said the smell was what stuck with her, what she remembered more than anything else. Said she'd take the memory of that horrible smell to her grave."

Beside them, Fortuna moaned. The ship rocked again on her mooring and the spars and yards creaked above. The *clink, clink* of mast hoops and pulleys echoed through the hold, as though reminding them that they weren't alone in the dark pit. That there were scores of others—souls who would not let their presence be forgotten.

"Pa," Fortuna moaned, "I'm sorry."

This brought Lucky back to the present. "You better be sorry, you dirty dog." Lucky kicked at the sound of Fortuna's voice, but only managed to bang his foot hard against the ladder.

"I don't think he can hear you," Daniel said.

"I'll try harder." Fortuna's voice sounded small, as though it belonged to a young boy.

"Try any harder and you may finish me off," Lucky spat the words into the stagnant air.

"Sounds like he's rememberin' some part of his past," Daniel said.

"Landlubber," Fortuna said miserably. "Not fit to change slop buckets."

Lucky straightened. *Not fit to change slop buckets.* He'd heard that phrase before. Pa'd used it to describe greenhands who couldn't get the hang of life at sea.

Lucky turned toward Daniel. "He's not talking to us, he's talking to my pa."

"Don't leave me, Pa! Didn't mean...break commandment #2," Fortuna mumbled.

"What's commandment #2?" Daniel asked.

"'Lie, but never about anything important'."

"Sounds like your pa could be pretty tough," Daniel said after a while.

Lucky nodded in the darkness. "Only when he drank." He added quickly, "But he didn't do that very often." Another thought occurred to him. "At least not while I was aboard with him."

"I'm sure your pa did the best he could with what he'd been given," Daniel said.

Lucky nodded absently. The father Fortuna spoke to in his dreams sure didn't sound much like the father Lucky knew. But the slop bucket comment was Pa, all right.

The smell and darkness pressed in on Lucky, making his forehead sweat and the bile rise in his throat. What if the Pa Lucky knew grew out of mistakes he'd made with Fortuna? Did that mean Lucky owed something to Fortuna, after all? He shook his head to banish the thought. But another one, even more disturbing, swam up to take its place. Could it be like Mrs. Cabral had said, that Fortuna was doing the best he could with what *he'd* been given?

Open Chain

L ucky worked the ropes around his wrists with Pa's
knife. *Do the best you can with what you've been given.*
Don't waste what you've learned. The phrases kept running through his head like the chorus of a tired sea chantey.

Having Pa's knife was a gift, that much was sure. But
what other gifts did Lucky possess? Emmeline's brooch. But
that wouldn't do him any good here; it'd only get taken.
Would anything he'd learned be enough to get them out of
here?

Finally, after nearly slicing his wrist more than a dozen
times, Lucky freed his hands from the ropes.

"You awake, Daniel?"

"Yes."

Lucky took his best reckoning of Daniel's position and
reached out in the dark.

"Aaargh!" Daniel cried and shifted violently. "Something
just touched my head!"

"Shhh! That was me."

"How did you—"

"I used what I'd been given. Pa's knife."

"Reckoned you'd lost it in the water," Daniel said. "One more thing I felt bad about, besides being too scared to jump when given the chance."

Suddenly, the hatch flew open.

Lucky jumped back into the shadow of the ladder, frantically searching the decking around him for the discarded rope.

A lantern shone into the dark recesses of the hold, and a moon-faced deckhand stuck his head through the opening.

Lucky sat next to Daniel, hiding his arms and the severed line behind his back, as though the bonds still held.

The sailor lumbered down the ladder, holding the lantern in front of him.

"Evening, ladies," he said. He prodded Fortuna with the toe of his shoe. "Not come to yet, huh? For the best, likely. He'll have an awful headache."

The deckhand walked past the mainmast, and the lantern illuminated a collection of casks and barrels that must have held the ship's stores. He stuck his head in a barrel.

"Don't worry about being lonely down here," he said, his voice muffled. He emerged with what appeared to be a few sprouted potatoes.

"Who's coming?" Lucky asked.

"More darkies, who else?"

"Where from?"

"Here and other ports." The deckhand leaned into another barrel and hit his head. A mumbled curse followed. "Look what you've made me do! And it's none of your business, anyway."

"I was just wondering, since Jessup said you'd been to Boston. Weren't you able to find any fugitives up there?"

The sailor squinted toward Lucky. "What d'ya know about Boston?"

"Nothing. Heard it's a rough place, though."

"Well, it was a bad business there, that's sure. A bunch of rabble-rousing know-nothings got all riled up. Before we knew it, them fugitives was gone."

"How do you know you won't find the same everywhere you go?" Lucky asked.

The man grunted. "Cap'n's got a network of spies all up and down the eastern seaboard. Providence to Philadelphia and beyond. Folks keeping tabs on the whereabouts of escaped slaves. Gathering 'em up will be like shooting fish in a barrel." He replaced the lid of the cask and pounded it in place with his fist.

Lucky and Daniel drew back into the shadows as he passed, but Lucky stole a glance at Fortuna. The lantern light exposed closed eyes and an open mouth.

"Don't worry, girls, there won't be any trouble from here on out," he said. "None of those fanatics will keep us from what we came for." He started up the ladder, but turned to smirk down at them. "We've got the law on our side this time."

When the hatch had closed again, Lucky and Daniel waited for a while in silence.

"We can't just jump overboard now," Lucky said as he started working on Daniel's ropes. "Jessup and the others will just sail on down to the next city and round up fugitives there. We have to do something more."

"What?"

Lucky thought for a moment. "We can stop this ship."

"What good will that do? They'll just get it going again."

"Not if we turn them in." Lucky breathed too deeply and gagged on the fetid air.

Daniel snorted. "Didn't you hear the man, they've got the law on *their* side."

"In one way, maybe," Lucky said, trying to remember something he'd heard on the *Nightbird*. "But even though the law says Jessup can come up here and get you and the others, I believe the law also says it's illegal to run a slave ship."

"Huh?"

"Those fancy lawyers in Washington made it illegal to bring new slaves from Africa into this country, but not illegal to fetch back into bondage the ones who were already here and escaped to a free state."

"Are you sure?"

"Heard tell of a slave ship getting boarded and taken up in New York not too long ago."

"Even if what you say is true," Daniel said after he'd thought about it for a moment, "how you gonna stop this ship?"

"*I'm* not. *We* are."

"How?"

"Here," Lucky said, handing Daniel the sliced rope that had bound his wrists. "By making the most of the gifts we've been given. Mine in rigging, and yours in spinning."

A moan from Fortuna startled them.

Not wanting to take the chance of his half brother hearing, Lucky leaned over and whispered his plan to Daniel.

"Well?" Lucky asked when he'd finished.

"Won't they have guards posted?"

"In port, it's called anchor watch," Lucky said. "One fore, one aft. 'Cept they're looking for folks coming *toward* the ship, not watching for someone already aboard."

Daniel swallowed audibly. "We'll jump overboard once we're done?" he asked.

"We need to wait until the ship's under way. Otherwise, they might suspect we've been about and caused some mischief. Besides, once they're under sail, it'll be near impossible for 'em to stop and catch us. We'll come back down here after we're done and make it look like we're still tied up. Then, when the ship starts moving, we'll climb out of the hold and jump off."

"That still leaves one big problem," Daniel said. "What if someone comes down here in the meantime? They see we're gone, and Jessup will comb the ship for us. Your plan won't work if anyone suspects."

"I hadn't thought of that," Lucky said, his spirits sinking.

"One of us needs to stay here and try to silence anyone who comes down."

"Won't work. We each need to do our part above deck."

They sat in a desperate and miserable silence, the heavy stench threatening to drive away all hope.

A voice cut like a jagged knife through the darkness. "I'll help you," Fortuna said.

Deadeye Lashing

Lucky flinched. He rubbed his eyes, as though it might help him find even the tiniest glimmer of light in the black stench of the hold. Nothing. The void pressed around him, making his chest ache. How much had Fortuna heard? Was his plan doomed to failure before they'd even started?

"Help us? Hear that, Daniel? Fortuna wants to help us!" Lucky grabbed at his gut, forgetting for a moment that no one could see his show of mock humor in the pitch dark of the hold. "Ouch." He'd clutched at the place where he'd fastened Emmeline's brooch and the pin pricked his thumb.

Silence.

"Daniel?"

"We *need* him," Daniel said quietly.

"He can't be trusted. I can't believe you'd consider—"

"We need him. If your plan is to have a chance, and I think it does, we need his help."

"How do we know he won't rat us out to Jessup?" Lucky reached up and traced the curved beams of the ship's hull.

"Why would he? We're *his* only chance, too, aren't we?"

"I don't like it."

"Way I see it, it's like you told me. We got to do the best we can with what we've been given. Fortuna's what we've been given."

Lucky thought about it for a moment. "Fortuna's no gift. More like a weight to bear. But I suppose you're right."

"Speaking of weight," Daniel said. "What about this dress?"

Lucky took out Pa's knife. "Hold still." He lifted the fabric of Daniel's skirt and made a cut just under the bodice. "My apologies for ruining your dress, Beulah," he said as the fabric tore.

"We're going aloft," Lucky told Fortuna. "You're to stay here and stop any member of the crew who comes down before we get back."

"Done." Fortuna said. "But you'll have to cut these ropes."

"Why would I do that? What's to keep you from climbing out of here? You could ruin the whole plan."

Fortuna blew out a breath. "I won't leave, but I can't fight with my hands tied."

"He's right," Daniel said.

"Trust me." Fortuna's voice was low and pleading. "I want off this ship as much as you do, probably more. But I want Jessup to get what he deserves. Besides, when have I ever lied to you?"

"You've cheated me," Lucky said. "Out of what's mine by rights."

"But when have I ever lied to you?"

Lucky's stomach had gone bilgy and his head ached. "Turn your back and hold out your wrists," he said.

Several hours later, when the footsteps above deck had quieted, Lucky climbed the ladder with Daniel close on his heels. At the top, he lifted the hatch a crack and listened. Nothing but the wind in the rigging. The ship rocked as they climbed onto the deck.

Lucky's hands itched to start up the ratlines. Though still dark and cloudy, dawn gathered strength in the eastern horizon. So little time! If they weren't able to finish before the mill whistle blew, it would be too late.

Carefully, he closed the hatch and stood on it for a moment. Could Fortuna be trusted? He didn't think so, but his plan wouldn't work if they didn't start right away. Lucky motioned to Daniel and they slid behind a small rowboat turned bottom up and lashed to the deck of the ship.

"See yonder light burning aft?" Lucky pointed. "Bet they're over there in the galley, but I'll go over and check."

"I'll go with you," Daniel whispered.

"No. Stay here and make sure Fortuna doesn't come up."

Daniel shook his head. "What am I supposed to do if he tries?"

"I dunno. Jump on the hatch."

"You're bluffing, Jessup! I call!" A shout came from the galley.

"Good, they're playing cards," Lucky said. "That should keep them occupied. I'll show you what you need to do. First, though, we should unlash this side of the dory, so we can get underneath." Lucky undid the jamming hitch knot that held one side, gave the line enough slack that they could raise the small boat enough to get under, then retied the rope, pushing the excess under the side. "That should do," he said. "If you need to get under, lift here." Daniel nodded.

They approached the mizzenmast. Lucky found a length of line attached to a cleat. He wrapped it around his arm and nodded, satisfied.

"What's that for?" Daniel whispered.

"We have but one knife," Lucky reminded him. "I'll take it up the mainmast, since I'll be quicker in climbing the ratlines. Once I'm done, I'll need to get it across to you."

"Why can't you just hand it to me?"

"We'll be fifty feet aloft, that's why."

Daniel stared at him, his mouth wide.

"You didn't think we could cut the rigging from the deck, did you?"

"Course not."

But Lucky could see from the way Daniel stared up at where the mainmast disappeared into the darkness, that it was exactly what he'd thought.

"Listen, if you can't do it, tell me now."

"I'll do it."

"Remember," Lucky said, "you need to weaken the rope, not sever it."

"Who taught you about thread strength?" Daniel asked,

letting the question dangle like bait on a hook.

"You," Lucky admitted.

A sudden crash cut through the wind and night.

"Quick, under the dory."

They rolled under the overturned boat just in time. Running footsteps came near and voices sounded on the deck.

"Check the hold," Jessup ordered.

"No need," another shouted. "Just a gull dropping a clam onto the deck."

Awk, awk.

Afraid to even breathe, Lucky and Daniel lay perfectly still.

After a few minutes, the men retreated and the deck was quiet again. "Dawn's just a shadow's breadth away," Lucky said. "Come on!" He peeked out from under the dory, and crawled onto the open deck. Once standing, he held the boat up so Daniel could follow. Together, they crept to the mizzenmast.

"It's one foot at a time, hand over fist," Lucky said as he showed Daniel how to get up the ratlines. Climbing rigging took practice, and Daniel would have to do it in the dark and wind. It was risky. But the ship was not under sail, so at least he wouldn't have to dodge moving parts. Lucky took a deep breath of sea air. They could not afford to fail.

"You all right?" he asked Daniel as he left him at the ratline that led up the mizzenmast.

"I'll keep."

"I'll wave my kerchief when I'm done and then I'll toss the knife across to you. Once you catch the line, tug on it to let me know you have the knife. I'll come down the mainmast and wait for you at the dory."

Daniel swallowed hard. "Aye, aye," he said.

Lucky left him and headed to the main, where he hoisted himself up the yard. He patted the smooth, solid bulk of the mast three times for luck, and began to climb.

The wind hissed through the yards and spars. Climbing the rigging was more difficult and took longer than Lucky had planned. Finally, he reached the lines he needed to weaken and started cutting. He could do it by feel, but worried that Daniel might not be able to do the same.

His eyes strayed to the lightening horizon and then the pier, where a lantern moved. He froze. There was a knock. In a moment, the galley door opened and Jessup came on deck. Lucky pressed against the mainmast, hoping to blend in with the dark wood. He scanned the mizzenmast for Daniel. His friend was halfway up and had obviously heard the commotion. Still as a statue, he hugged the mizzenmast.

Jessup approached the side of the ship and looked down onto the wharf. What could this be? Lucky wondered. The man holding the lantern called something up to Jessup, but his words were too muffled for Lucky to make out.

Whatever he'd said had made Jessup as angry as a harpoon in the eye. His voice became louder and louder until his words carried clear up into the night.

"What do you mean, they're gone? All of them?"

The visitor shifted his feet on the wharf and took his cap. Lucky couldn't hear his response.

"I've spent too much time and too much money in these God-forsaken parts to come away with nothing!"

The fugitives must have made it out safely!

Lucky glanced over at Daniel and then to the eastern sky. He'd already reached the right spot in the rigging, but would there be time enough to do the deed?

Once finished, Lucky let out the breath he'd been holding. He ran a hand along the lines he'd been working on. Cords fell away beneath his touch. Had his cuts been just the right depth? Too much, and the lines would split too soon, and be replaced. Too little, and lines might hold, leaving the slave ship to continue on its journey south, gathering more and more fugitives.

So much was tied up in this web of hemp and cordage.

Lucky uncoiled the length of rope he'd found on deck and tied the knife to one end in a secure monkey claw. Then, he removed Pa's kerchief from his neck and shook it in the direction of the mizzenmast. He thought he could make out the black of Daniel's bodice against the slack white of the sail.

He tossed the monkey claw and cringed when he heard the knife clatter against the mast. He tried again, but it came back with a *whoosh*, hitting the mainsail below him. Lucky gazed up at the sky. While they'd been working, dawn had crept onto the eastern horizon.

Finally, on the third try, Daniel caught the rope and reeled in the knife. Lucky felt a tug before the line dropped back to him. He coiled it around his arm and descended slowly onto the ship's deck and made his way back to the dory. And waited.

Daniel was taking too long! Lucky peered out from under the boat, wishing he could see the sky. Something must have gone wrong. A vision of his friend caught in the rigging like a fish in a net flashed through Lucky's head. He listened hard, but could hear nothing over the clank of the pulleys and the creak of the masts. He was just about to risk leaving his cover and running over to the mizzenmast when a piercing screech cut the air.

The mill whistle!

And in that moment, the dory lifted slightly and Daniel slid in next to him. Just in time, for they could already hear the footsteps of the crew on deck. Heavy treads advanced toward their hiding place.

The toes of two leather boots appeared in the opening under the skiff. Lucky felt the deck begin to vibrate, but then realized it was Daniel lying beside him, shaking like a tub of blubber.

"Look," one of the deckhands shouted. "Over there!"

The boots moved away from the dory and toward the port side of the ship.

"What in the blue blazes...?" Jessup said.

Waterman's Knot

Lucky pushed his face against the smooth deck and peered out from under the dory. "There's a crowd of people coming over the bridge."

"Let me see."

He moved so Daniel could look. Already the hum of voices echoed over the water.

"They're coming down the wharf. I can't believe—"

"Who?" Lucky pushed to get a look.

"Workers from the mill!"

A gull cried overhead. Delph?

"What business have you here?" the captain called down to the crowd assembling on the wharf.

"We'd ask the same of you, sir." Lucky thought he recognized the voice of the abolitionist speaker at the antislavery meeting.

"In port to supply my ship for a whaling voyage," the captain said. "Not that it's any of your affair."

"We have reason to believe otherwise, and ask your permission for several of our number to board and search your ship."

"Permission denied," Jessup's high voice rang out.

"You stand accused of waylaying lawful citizens of this district," the abolitionist leader called.

"'Tis a fact!" came Emmeline's voice.

"My boarder, Lucky Valera, went missing last night." Mrs. Cabral!

"And two of our number, mulespinners at the mill." The crowd clamored and pressed in.

"We mean to search this ship!" the stevedore shouted.

"You'll do no such thing," Jessup snapped.

"Then you'll neither leave this ship, nor have any supplies or provisions delivered."

Lucky felt a slight shift of the deck beneath them. "The captain's preparing to sail," he whispered to Daniel.

The attention of the crowd seemed to have turned. A hush fell as the sound of hoofbeats got closer, then stopped nearby. A horse whinnied.

"Thornton Jessup, you are a known kidnapper, recently thwarted from going about your evil business on the streets of Boston," called a deep voice Lucky didn't recognize.

"Who are you to make such an accusation?" the captain demanded.

"I am Abermarle Mayhew of the Boston Vigilance Committee." Lucky sucked in a breath. Emmeline's uncle!

"Mayhew!" Jessup voice was a sneer. "Unlike you, I'm a law-abiding citizen. I am authorized by the law to retrieve stolen property from these parts. Harboring fugitive slaves is against the law. The Fugitive Slave Law says I'm allowed to collect them."

"You'll find no satisfaction on these shores, Jessup. Most of the fugitives you seek have made safely away to Canada. You'll hand over the others or not be permitted to leave this port."

"That's what you think, Mayhew." Jessup drew a pistol from his belt. "Any of you touches this ship, and I'll fire in self defense."

"Hold the lines!" someone shouted. "They mean to flee."

"Now," Lucky said.

But when they tried to lift the dory, it wouldn't budge. Someone was standing firmly on the gunwale, trapping them. There came a shuffling sound, and darkness engulfed them as a sail came down over their hiding place!

"Help!" Lucky cried.

"Here!" Daniel called.

"Cap'n Mayhew," they yelled together, but already Lucky could feel the ship in motion, slipping her lines and surging toward the mouth of the harbor amid the shouts of the onlookers.

"Look," a woman's voice cried above the din. "It's a fugitive!"

A large splash followed.

Lucky turned to Daniel. "That would be Fortuna."

"They say rats leave a sinking ship," Daniel offered.

"He can't swim," a woman yelled. "Somebody fetch him out!"

There was commotion on the wharf.

Lucky shot up, his head hitting the side of the dory. Could it be that the mighty Fortuna didn't know how to swim?

188

The voices on shore dimmed as the ship quit the harbor. The currents ran hard.

Light appeared as the dory was lifted off Lucky and Daniel. "What have we here?" Jessup's smile was tight.

"We should have left them, Jessup!" the captain said. "Why didn't you tell me they were still aboard before we sailed?"

"I have unfinished business with this one," Jessup said, the toe of his boot jabbing at Daniel. Lucky peered over to see that his friend's face had gone expressionless again.

The captain cursed under his breath. "They're bad luck. We should set 'em adrift in that dory."

But Jessup wasn't having it. Instead, the boys were bound again and returned to the hold.

For a long time, Lucky and Daniel crouched back-to-back in the dark. Whether from an empty stomach, the pitch blackness, or a combination of the two, Lucky's guts heaved with each surge and sway of the ship.

Lucky figured that it had been more than an hour since they'd left New Bedford. Though the wind was stiff and the sails full, the rigging still held.

"I must not have cut deep enough," Lucky said, keeping his head between his knees.

"Probably my fault," Daniel offered. "I'm not as good with a knife as you are."

"It's not your fault! I was the one with the fool idea."

"Cutting the rigging was a fine idea."

"It was all for nothing."

"Not for nothing. We did the best we could with what—"

"I know, I know," Lucky said. "But it wasn't enough."

"We did the best we could. Least we can look back with a clear conscience."

"I guess you're right, but that won't do us much good where we're going."

They sat in silence and Lucky wondered at the feel of the ship gliding through the waves, the gentle sway of the hull and the sound of the wind in the sails. He felt for Emmeline's brooch, still pinned to the inside of the bodice, and realized he'd not get the chance to return it to her as he'd dreamed of doing. Would he ever even see Emmeline again? His throat ached and he rubbed the pin against his thumb to distract his thoughts. But it was no use. The knot of gold felt brittle and warm, accusing.

"You all right?" Daniel asked.

"You could have jumped when you'd climbed back down from the mizzenmast. Why didn't you?" Lucky said.

"Why didn't *you*?"

"Job wasn't done yet."

"Not done."

BOOM! The hold vibrated with a hot and hollow sound. Then came a tremendous splash from the starboard side. Lucky and Daniel sat straight up, bumping heads. A cannon!

The ship changed tack and they braced against each others backs to keep their balance.

"Do you think?" Lucky asked but then hushed to better hear the voices above deck.

"They're gaining!" Jessup shouted.

"Loosen the battens and hoist the jibs," the captain called. "Ready on the braces."

"Faster, you idiots!" Jessup yelled.

"We can outrun them," the captain cried. "We're the faster ship!"

"You'd better be right. We've fugitives to collect in Providence come nightfall."

"I've more at stake than you, Jessup! I'll lose my ship if they come onboard and find we're a slaver. You should have let them boys go! This is a problem of your making!"

All of a sudden, there was a loud ripping sound followed by a bone-jarring thud.

Lucky jumped to his feet. "Could it be?" He strained to hear what was going on above deck, his legs tensed for clues in the movement of the ship.

"What in the name of—" the captain shouted above. "The rigging on the mainsail's failed!"

Already the boat had slowed. Daniel let out a low whistle.

"Pull in the mizzen, boys, pull for all you're worth!" the captain shouted.

Another crash made the deck vibrate.

"The mizzen's gone, too, Cap'n!"

Lucky's chest felt full enough to burst. They'd done it! "Did you hear that?" he said.

"What is it?" Daniel asked.

"The sound of freedom."

Ending Rope

Lucky stared out from the crow's nest at the vast expanse of sea. Relishing the feel of the ship's movement below his feet and the gentle rocking of the mast beside him, he closed his eyes for a moment and listened to the creak of the rigging and the wind catching the sails.

He took a breath of salt-tinged air. It tasted sweeter and richer than he remembered. Mayhap it wasn't that the air was different, Lucky thought, but that he had changed curing the time he'd spent with the landlubbers.

The word made him pause. It was hard to think of the people he'd met, those he'd become close to, in the same terms anymore. The lines that separated him from others had frayed and unraveled like the ropes on Jessup's ship. And suddenly the differences between those who took to the sea and those who lived on land seemed far less important than the things they had in common.

Was that honeysuckle he smelled? Lucky peered portside as the rooftops and chimneys of New Bedford disappeared behind him. He tried to catch a glimpse of Cannon Street and Mrs. Cabral's boardinghouse, but the sails had caught the wind and the streets faded into the distance. He'd promised to visit when he got back to port. The landlady had just grinned and reminded him that she could always use a hand.

A gull's cry brought his attention back to the ship. Three birds flew past the starboard rail, none of them Delph. He hadn't seen his friend since the *Perseverance* had docked in New Bedford with the disabled slave ship in tow and Jessup, its captain, and crew in irons. He could still hear the cheers of the crowd gathered on the wharf and feel the hands reaching out to shake his own.

Lucky scanned the decks below. A fine ship she was; every bit as fine as the *Nightbird*. He reckoned his old ship would have already have already rounded the Horn and be halfway to the Marquesas by now. He felt a pang and knew he'd miss his old crewmates and the rush of the hunt. But there'd be no more chasing the *Nightbird*; at least not for the time being. There was more important work to be done.

Here on the *Perseverance* there'd be no searching the horizon for spouts—her whaleship fittings were just a clever disguise, allowing her to pass easily in and out of any port without attracting extra attention. Lucky took a deep breath. If all went as planned, the ship would soon be carrying a cargo far more precious than whale oil: fugitive slaves on their way to freedom.

The spray off the starboard bow glistened like a thousand precious jewels in the morning sun. Portside, a school of porpoises leapt and cavorted, keeping pace with the ship as it cut through the waves, heading south.

"Ahoy!"

"Ahoy," Lucky called back down the mainmast to the figure below. Then, humming one of the chanteys he'd learned from Pa, he shimmied down the ratlines, jumping the last few feet to the deck.

"With this wind, we'll make Baltimore in no time," Daniel said as Lucky closed the distance between them.

"Sorry you're not on your way to Canada?" Lucky asked.

"Nah. But I'd never have dreamed I'd be trying my luck as a greenhand."

"I'm grateful Fortuna headed to Lowell without me. Said I was more trouble than I was worth."

"What do you think will become of him?"

"He'd never make it as a sailor, that's sure."

"You think that's why he and your pa fell out?"

"Likely. It was the only life Pa knew." Lucky shook his head. "Maybe Fortuna will get rich one of these days." He sighed. "Don't envy him that, though. All the riches in the world won't make you happy if you've got no anchor. That's what Pa said."

"Anchor?"

"A powerful belief or faith. Something that keeps you from drifting about hither and yon."

"What about Miss Alice?"

Lucky shook his head. "I don't think another person can be your anchor. Besides, I wouldn't bet on her putting up with his shenanigans for long."

"Don't believe you'll be doing any betting, anyway," Daniel said. "Word is, Captain Mayhew runs a tight ship.

That new tutor's powerful strict as well—Miss Emmeline says he'll soon have us all talking like books."

"Could be worse," Lucky said. "At least it's not Miss Patience Pritwell's School for Young Ladies of Quality."

"Ahem," came a voice from behind them. Emmeline curtsied deeply as she stepped from behind the mainmast. "One can never have too much quality."

"True." Lucky laughed. "Did you talk to the captain? Are you sure you have to go to Philadelphia?"

"We could use your help with the fugitives," Daniel said.

"Aunt Mayhew is waiting for me." Emmeline smiled. "I may not be able to go all the way to Baltimore with thee, but there are other ways I can aid the cause." She touched the strands of the knotted brooch at her throat.

"Sounds like you have a plan," Lucky said.

"I do. I've been gathering the stories of fugitives and putting them to paper. I'm going to ask Aunt Mayhew's help in getting them published."

"Fugitives like me?" Daniel asked.

"I'm hoping thou will tell me thy story before we dock next week," Emmeline said shyly.

"Be proud to," he said.

Awwwk. Awwwk.

This time when Lucky glanced up, it was Delph's dark head that tilted toward him from one of the spars on the mainmast.

"Where've you been?" he called to the gull.

"I believe she's come to give us her blessing," Daniel said.

"And to wish us well on our journeys," Emmeline added.

"You think we're up for it?"

"Pray we are," Daniel said. "Lots of folks counting on us."

"Getting that ship out of Baltimore will be the trickiest bit of sailing I've ever had a hand in."

Awwk, awwk!

"I think Delph likes our chances," Lucky said.

The gull eyed him steadily, and it seemed to Lucky that she winked before taking off. She glided toward the horizon, feathers shimmering brighter and brighter until there was no telling them from the sun-touched waves.

Author's Note

Although the characters in the story are fictitious, many elements of *Chasing the Nightbird* are based on historical fact. Mid-nineteenth-century New Bedford was an ethnically and culturally diverse city and home to Cape Verdeans, Quakers, and fugitive slaves.

Even before the Revolutionary War, whaleships were picking up crew on the Cape Verde Islands. When New Bedford became the hub of the whaling industry, Cape Verdeans started immigrating to the city. Though they tended to live in their own neighborhoods, it wasn't until later in the nineteenth century that they formed a significant proportion of the workforce in New Bedford's textile mills.

Of the over 700 whaling ships in existence in the 1840s, New Bedford was home port for more than 400. It became known as "The City that Lit the World" and grew rich supplying whale oil for lamps and spermaceti (a liquid wax that came from the sperm whale) for candles. Wealthy captains and merchants built mansions on the hill above the harbor.

Many of these captains and ship owners were Quakers, who believe all people are created equal in the eyes of God.

Quakers took an early stand against slavery and were influential in founding the abolitionist movement. This helped to make the whaling industry and New Bedford a haven for fugitive slaves.

It's hard to imagine Quakerism being compatible with the authentic whalemen's commandments Lucky lives by in the story. But whalemen also played an important role in the abolitionist movement. A racially and culturally diverse group, the nature and difficulty of their work led to judgments of each other based on ability rather than skin color.

Frederick Douglass escaped slavery using sailor's protection papers given to him by a friend. When he arrived in New Bedford in 1838, he found people of color "much more spirited than I had supposed they would be. I found among them a determination to protect each other from the bloodthirsty kidnapper, at all hazards."

There are documented cases of attempted kidnappings of fugitives from the city. In 1851 the bell at Liberty Hall was rung to warn of the approach of federal marshals sent to enforce The Fugitive Slave Act of 1850, which made it illegal to harbor an escaped slave. The law further mandated that anyone suspected of being a runaway slave could be arrested without warrant and turned over to a claimant on nothing more than his sworn testimony of ownership. Also, a suspected black slave could not ask for a jury trial nor testify on his or her behalf. Despite this law, no fugitive is ever known to have been returned to slavery from New Bedford.

From the mid-1840s to 1860 between 300 and 700 fugitive slaves lived in New Bedford.

While some escaped by ship, others, like Daniel in the story, used directions they heard in songs such as "Follow the Drinking Gourd" to travel north on foot. Still others were led to New Bedford by conductors on the Underground Railroad, such as Harriet Tubman, who also spent time in New Bedford.

Other elements of the story, including whaleships outfitted as slave ships (as Jessup's ship was) and the attempted rescue of slaves by ship (as Lucky and Daniel set off to do in the end) are also based on documented accounts.

Below is a list of my main sources.

Blockson, Charles L. *The Underground Railroad: First Person Narratives of Escapes to Freedom in the North*. New York: Prentice Hall, 1987.

Church, Albert Cook. *Whale Ships and Whaling*. New York: Bonanza Books, 1938.

Cohn, Michael and Michael K. H. Platzer. *Black Men of the Sea*. New York: Dodd, Mead & Company, 1978.

Grover, Kathryn. *The Fugitives Gibraltar: Escaping Slaves and Abolitionism in New Bedford, Massachusetts*. Amherst: University of Massachusetts Press, 2001.

Grover, Kathryn. "Fugitive Slave Traffic and the Maritime World of New Bedford." *A Research Paper prepared for New*

Bedford Whaling Historic Park and the Boston Support Office of the National Park Service, 1998.

Lobban, Richard A., Jr. *Cape Verde: Crioulo Colony to Independent Nation.* Boulder: Westview Press, 1995.

McKissack, Patricia C. and Fredrick L. *Black Hands, White Sails: The Story of African-American Whalers.* New York: Scholastic Press, 1999.

Michaels, Susan (Producer), Woodard, Alfre (Host). (2002). *Underground Railroad: A New documentary that unveils the history heroes and villains of the Abolitionist movement.* [VHS], New York: The History Channel.

Thompson, Warren E. "Kidnappings in the North." *Spinner: People and Culture in Southeastern Massachusetts,* Vol IV, (1988), p. 69.

Note: The knots pictured on the chapter opener pages came from *Knots, Splices, and Rope Work* by A. Hyatt Verrill, first published in 1917 and released in 2004 as eBook #13510 by Project Gutenberg.

ACKNOWLEDGMENTS

Many thanks to Jessica Alexander, my editor at Peachtree, who believed in this project from the start and worked tirelessly to bring it to life with brilliant ideas and suggestions. Also to Marian Gordin and Vicky Holifield for their amazing copyediting, Mo Withee for her spectacular cover design, and all the folks at Peachtree who lent their expertise to this book.

To Carol Lee Lorenzo, for her longtime support and mentoring, and the other members of my critique group: Joy Pope-Alandete, Sandy Fry, Kit Robey and Kelly Williams.

Also to Tim Esaias, Leslie Davis Guccione, Anne Harris, Kristi Holl, and the faculty and staff of Seton Hill University's WPF Program.

I especially want to thank Kathryn Grover for her book *The Fugitives Gibraltar: Escaping Slaves and Abolitionism in New Bedford, Massachusetts* and Patricia C. and Fredrick L. McKissack for *Black Hands, White Sails: The Story of African-American Whalers.* These important works inspired me and I returned to them again and again. Of course, any errors made in interpreting the history therein are my own.